TIN MOON

BLAKELY CHORPENNING

Cover design by JJ's Design & Creations
Formatting by Inked Imagination Services
Editing by Faith Williams of The Atwater Group

DEDICATIONS

To my mom, dad, daughter, husband, and mother-in-law. Nothing compares to the world we have together.

To Mom and Aunt Lee. You have taught me that strength, as a woman, is self-defined. It comes in many forms and choices. Thank you for always seeing my strengths and supporting my choices, regardless of if they are wackadoo sometimes.

To those who left not long ago and never seem far from our hearts:
Shirley K., Dorothy C., Ann W., Aaron G., Judith G., Bruce A., Beverly S., Dennis S., Renee S., and Bree B.

Not a day without you.
Not one.

And to those who live well in your own skin, faults be damned. Thank you for being you.

ACKNOWLEDGMENTS

A special thank you to Mrs. Mabel Catherine Allen Harris. Without your wonderful life accounts, finding the feel of early twentieth-century Granville County would have been nearly impossible. I am forever grateful.

Thank you Jeannette, Rebecca, Colleen, and Danielle for being the best damned friends a woman could ask for. You all shine, making the world beautifully complicated with your brilliance and a little wild with your spirit.

Bree, your absence has left a room in my heart that I visit often, sometimes quietly, sometimes furiously. I am thankful for this space because it makes me realize that you are so much more than a memory. It is my proof that you were here, that you will always be here. Thank you for being my friend.

PROLOGUE

I never had nothing important to say, but my time on this dirt rather than in it makes me wish my secrets had wings to lift me up. I don't know where they might take me. They spent plenty of years dragging me down.

My name is Nora Cravis, and I never left Granville County more than one day in my whole life. But my heart's traveled farther than the devil's laughter and shivered under the heat.

CHAPTER ONE

No Place Like Home
1917

*M*y family's tobacco farm was a fine playground as a child. There were a number of tobacco barns on our property to hide inside. Each barn was four rooms in size. Not everyone had that many rows for drying. If I stood just right, I could line up the oak cladding boards in my sightline until they mashed together to create one massive wall.

Surrounded by row after row of seven-foot stalks, our house sat a hundred yards away in a thinned grove of trees, nothing but dirt all around. We had a large woodstove to wrap us tight through cold nights, and a covered porch the size of our beloved North Carolina to shade our over-heated bodies when the temperatures boiled the mercury right out of the thermometer. It wasn't much to no one else, but Daddy had taken a run-down state of nothing and birthed life into it like women birth babies into the world. As children, it taught us the value of sweat. More so, it taught me that home was a process.

James, Dewey, and Able, my older brothers, never let our

father work alone. If he was putting his boots on, they made sure their laces were already tied. If he was one foot out the door, they were two ahead of him. And they were forever nagging me to be worth more than the corn I ate or the tobacco I pulled. No matter my workload, nothing ever seemed to placate their concerns. Not minding that a Carolina summer felt like the palm of Hell. Or that I was a string bean compared to my brothers, and didn't have the length or muscles to keep up with them. My hands could be raw, the leaves stacked higher than the hair on God's head, and they'd demand more. There was no right in their eyes, so I cultivated my own pace and learned to block out their griping.

Still, watching them work alongside the tenant farmers year by year filled my heart up with pure home. The aroma of pinched tomato and green bean leaves, cow manure, and human will expelling from every pore in every body were among just a few of the smells that came together in the most perfect of ways.

Listening to my brothers hum and breathe, I enjoyed running between the shacks where they readied the tobacco for curing. This was a favored pastime well into my teens. If I laid on the ground and looked to the very peaks of the roofs, I imagined that's what it was like to walk down the streets of a city, saddled by buildings that stretched and kissed the sky. My Aunt Virgie had a notebook full of paintings and sketches of such buildings. She let me sneak across the field and hide away with it in her pantry whenever I asked, even as the pantry shrunk and my body hunched a little more with each passing year.

Of course, that meant I wasn't worth much at home. By seventeen, I was underwhelming, to say the least.

In the horse barn one day, his sweaty dark hair stuck to his forehead as James reminded me for the umpteenth time, "Daddy don't farm to keep you fed for nothin'."

Exasperated by his irritable temper, I snapped, "It's not like I'm eating the field bare. I don't weigh ninety pounds wet."

I never forgot the seriousness in his brow when he stopped working and turned to me, the stress of the tools over his shoulder pulling his skin every which way.

"Ninety pounds can sink any man."

James was an old twenty. He'd always been old. Somewhere, his youth had passed in the night like a ghost sneaking to Rapture. And damn him for making me feel naïve because I didn't want mine to pass by just as shameful.

That was the last real conversation I shared with James before marrying Rathe Cravis that summer. It was so small, but those words haunted me.

Ninety pounds can sink any man.

I never forgave him for putting upon my heart a weight greater than the tools he bore that day. Not then, not now. And it was, in part, this feeling that I couldn't do right that led me to the decision of becoming Mrs. Cravis.

It was inevitable that I would leave my daddy's house one day. Leave, find my place at the head of a new household, and bring my own babies into this green paradise. Something nagged at me, though. It tugged from deep inside, whispering, taunting me. *Could I be someone's wife?* I couldn't be trusted to feed the dern horses or keep track of my own shoes without constant reminding. I didn't always brush my hair, and my dresses had rips in them from climbing trees.

Oh dear, Mrs. Cravis...

But the day did ripen, and all fell into place as it should. I was to be Rathe Cravis's wife. My daddy had quite a few conversations with Rathe leading up to this day, mostly private. On a few occasions, however, I caught words such as "eternal" and "pig-headed." Rathe never spoke. He nodded a lot, and I suspected Daddy was threatening that he better treat me right because he didn't want me returned. Daddy and my younger sister, Shailene, had an innate affection that blossomed just by being close. Daddy and I, on the other hand, were as copasetic as two squirrels fighting for a lone walnut before the first frost.

So it was put into motion that I would go my own way. That way came awful fast, too.

"Are you ready, baby?" Momma tugged at my white cotton dress and tightened the sash around my waist. She saw my hands shaking and grinned. "He's a good boy. You done good. Made the right decision for once in your life. I don't know how you found time to catch someone's eye, spending all your time running between tobacco barns and overgrown paths your brothers made in the woods."

"I made my own paths, Momma."

"Oh," she tsk-tsked, "ain't no path hadn't been walked a hundred times before. Only Eve laid the first steps. Now," she grinned, "get out there before he changes his mind."

Momma meant well. She always meant well. It just never settled right with me. Maybe it was my fault. I'd always been awkward.

Nodding, I rubbed the bit of lace sewn to the white cotton dress, wondering whether Momma had added it just for me or whether it had been requested by Cousin Adelaide when she wore it last spring. I hadn't paid much attention then. Either way, it was the most delicate dress I expected to ever wear, and I appreciated each moment it swooshed over my pale legs.

Shailene popped through the door like a corn kernel and bounded into me. "Everyone's here, Sissy," she squealed. "They're all here for you." A kind of sparkle torched her words. She made being me sound special.

There wasn't a passing day that Shailene didn't find something absolutely moving to discuss with me. It drove our brothers batty some days, but I dearly enjoyed her observations. She had a particular way of capturing the life in something as she spoke of it.

I kissed the top of her head and wished she could stay twelve forever. We had never been a night apart, and I wondered just how fast she would grow when I wasn't around to witness every moment. Her round face would slowly start to thin and maybe those freckles on her nose would fade away into womanhood. Before the idea of her youth fleeing into the glory of life took hold of my thoughts, I noticed her rosy dress.

"You and Momma match."

Momma had cut their dresses from the same bolt of fabric.

"I know. Ain't I grown up?" Shailene came dangerously close to twirling on my bare feet, but I laughed.

"Stop, now," Momma warned. "It's Sissy's big day. Pull your hair back and take these." Momma handed her a bunch of wildflowers and tugged Shailene's waist-length hair into a perfect ponytail. It looked like a chestnut waterfall.

Momma turned to me, nose crinkled. "What have you done to your hair?"

"I brushed it." Subconsciously, my fingers combed through my thin, blonde hair.

"Did you wash it?"

"Yes, Momma. I washed it this morning."

Her eyes narrowed as her voice grew pointed. "Nora May, the angels above will descend and strike you down for lying!"

"Yesterday. I washed it yesterday, Momma." I stared at the floor before daring to meet her gaze.

"What shall we do with you? You're awkward and plain, and you lie like your daddy."

"I don't know, Momma."

Whenever I didn't know how to respond to my mother, this was my answer. She heard this phrase more often than the Eastern whippoorwill sang its incessant melody outside our kitchen window at dusk, because I never had the right words. I guess I didn't feel I needed them.

Shailene swished her dress between us, looked up, and proclaimed, "You're not plain. You're beautiful."

Momma managed a grin. "Out of the mouth of babes. Nora, you look beautiful." She grabbed my shoulders, hugged me, and whispered, "No one'll notice your hair."

"Is it time?" Shailene pestered.

"Let's have a wedding," Momma announced.

I turned to my little sister's moon-shaped face and said, "Wish on a star for me tonight."

The pepper-gray bun on Momma's head bounced as she gathered up every last bit of excitement and opened the door. Shooing Shailene first, she held the door, waiting on me. "One thing your grand-momma taught me...don't keep a good man waiting long or he just might find a good woman."

Her loud chuckle cut through the air.

Smiling, I grabbed her hand. "I'm glad you're here, Momma."

"Where else would I be, baby? Now get out there before your daddy thinks you run off."

"I'm going, I'm going."

I smiled, grateful to hug Momma one last time before walking up the wide, inviting steps into the warm embrace of Banks Methodist Church. Momma's family's church. I had spent more than my share of hours praying, fretting, and celebrating here. And now it was full again, but this time my family and friends, sweating shoulder to shoulder in the pews, were here for me and Rathe. For the bride and the groom, on one of the most beautiful days I never expected to have.

Preacher Smith, a man on the cusp of being too young for such a thin coat of hair and too old for such a peachy complexion, had come from the seminary in Wake Forest that Friday morning. Momma had made up my and Shailene's room for him. I guess it was just Shailene's room now. She expected him to eat a decent supper and sleep a fit night far away from the raucous festivities that would be considered unsuitable for a man of his position. In all honesty, I think the revelers-to-be feared having to answer for the sin of gluttony if such a holy witness existed.

Rathe stood to the side of the preacher, clasping his hands together to keep from wiping sweaty palms on his only pair of good pants. I knew they were his only pair, because not many folks around here had more than one good pair. He was dressed in his best collar shirt and looked no more a grown man than I looked a grown woman, though he was a full three years older than me.

Short, dark waves clung to his forehead, which glistened a bit with perspiration. It didn't detract from his natural handsomeness. Between his soft hair, impressive height, and muscles earned from days upon days of honest work, no

God anywhere could make two of him, seeing as how all the best material was used right here.

Walking down the aisle to stand by Rathe's side, a shiver shook my soul, and that thought crossed my mind again. *Am I good enough for this man?*

There was no fitting into someone else's skin to be who everyone wanted me to be. That was never an option, though I'd wished many times to be what they needed me to be in order not to fail them. If it were up to me, I'd never change me at all. If I lived on my own, far from their tongue-lashings and disappointed expressions, I expect I would have felt much lighter, and my thin skin wouldn't scald my heart half as often.

Looking up, staring into Rathe's blue eyes, if any there were a time to be everything for one person, I wanted it. I wanted to be the "her" that set the table every meal, made quilts to cuddle under, and knew just what to say to heal a hard day.

Almost swept away by wishes, I blinked as Rathe turned his attention to me, smiling. His smile, a genuine anomaly that seemed to come so easy and free, reached the creases of his eyes. I knew then, our home would never be cold.

Rathe managed that smile the entire ceremony, and that was saying a lot. Preacher Smith talked on and on about butterflies and baby's feet and God. I thought he'd never shut his trap and we'd all be standing there till one of us left in a casket. And when he addressed the duties of a wife, I wanted to die right there and sink into a crack in the floor-boards. How could I ever look my daddy in the eyes after a declaration like that?

In the stillness of the church, someone cleared his throat —my daddy, I was assuming—and Preacher Smith's eyes rounded just a little bit as he hurriedly changed the direction of his speech.

"Alone, we are but humble sinners. Together, we have the power to become more. We are concerned siblings, dutiful parents, attentive friends, sympathetic strangers. How do husband and wife fit into this tapestry, you may wonder. As kindred hearts, once strangers, you will build upon friendship to create new life and love."

Daddy mumbled, "I'm building a fist for the next person to mention baby-making."

Preacher Smith's eyes bulged. Shutting the Bible in his hands, which held his notes, he announced, "In front of God and the fellowship of this church, you are now man and wife. Kiss your bride, son."

Before Rathe could attempt Preacher Smith's final instruction, Daddy cleared his throat again and Rathe anxiously settled for a kiss that grazed the corner of my mouth.

Everyone clapped, and I heard Daddy say, "Praise God, she made it outta my house."

Rathe shook Daddy's hand. "Thank you, sir. I'll treat her good."

"Oh, I know you will."

In a tone I'd learned to decipher growing up, I knew Daddy's simple words were a threat, and something inside my heart glowed. My daddy loved me. He may not have been able to stand me, but he surely loved me.

Taking the opportunity, Momma tugged Rathe away from Daddy and pulled him along as she rustled the guests outside to eat. He turned to find me in the crowd. There was that smile again. Something about it put me right at ease. The wave of people shoving me out the back door seemed little more than a harsh wind in the presence of that smile.

The power it wielded astonished me. And thrilled me. There had never been nothing like it in my world.

My only regret was that Rathe's family couldn't be with us to see how happy their son was. To see that smile, to understand just how much I looked forward to seeing it every day from that moment forward. I'd only met them twice, briefly. Farmers from Virginia. Time was different for farmers, though. I knew that as well as any. Not much was worth stopping for, certainly not a wedding. The spirit could celebrate, as long as bodies dern well kept moving, because the land was awfully demanding. At times, it drained all hope and laughter, replacing it with pain or numbness, until there was no thinking. Bare feelings, remains of being human, traced our outlines but never quenched our souls. Those times, when the land became master, slave, child, and parent, were consuming because without it...we lost everything we loved.

Still, it would have been nice to start our life together in the presence of all our loved ones. I made sure to dance extra for Rathe's family and hoped the excitement and joy would reach their spirits across the many fields and stars that separated us.

Through the celebratory noise and frantic dancing throughout the evening, Shailene would often appear from the depths of the crowd to wrap her arms around my waist and hug like it was our last. It wasn't, of course. But it was our last as children. After all, I was someone's wife now. I would be sleeping in a room with a man rather than a little sister. In a year's time, I might have a child of my own, even.

I held back the tears that wanted to spill on top of Shailene's silky head of hair.

Before saying goodnight, I pulled Shailene aside and

whispered, "My heart doesn't know distance. It will love you just the same, no matter where I am."

That night, when our feet were worn from dancing and the men were so full of moonshine their eyelids refused to open, I carried my suitcase and presents to Rathe's wagon, and we started our trip down the dark, winding roads home, though I'd never been there before.

CHAPTER TWO

Star Light, Star Bright

*E*ven under the moonlight, it was beautiful. On top of the greenest hill sat a thin, shy, two-story house with a well-proportioned covered porch, perfect in every way. White like a candle cutting through the darkness. I didn't care that Rathe's hands had rebuilt it with another woman in mind two years prior. It was mine now.

"What do you think?" Rathe helped me from the wagon and stood by my side, trying not to care what my answer might be.

But I could hear him holding his breath.

"It's like a crown on the head of a queen."

His nose crinkled. "Is that...good?"

"It's a fairy tale," I whispered.

Only, in a fairy tale, the lovers kiss and the story ends. But we weren't kissing behind the tobacco barn or holding hands in church. We were married now.

Turning to him, I said, "If there could be something better than perfect, this would be just that."

I toured the house. *My* house. The living room was large enough for company and cozy enough for family. It smelled like the wood stove in the corner. Nothing a bit of mint couldn't help. The little white kitchen lacked adequate cabinet space. Momma wouldn't care much for it, but I appreciated the extra shelves for canning. They had never been used. The paint was still crisp, waiting for someone to shout, "I need you something awful." And there was a window right over the countertop, where I could look out over the patch of wildflowers we had passed on the way in. It was definitely something special.

There were two bedrooms upstairs. I quietly unpacked my suitcase into the right side of dresser drawers in the large bedroom, obvious by the blankets on the bed and lamp on the night table that this is where Rathe slept. It didn't take me long, and the modest drawers were left wanting because I didn't have much. Of course, I already had everything I needed. It just didn't seem real until this moment.

Opening the drawers on the left, I touched the coarse material of Rathe's shirts folded inside, if you could call that mess folded. An overwhelming need to pick them up and smell them swept over me. Maybe it was the need to make sure I wasn't dreaming. I didn't, however, because I heard him ascending the stairs.

I shut the drawer and turned, running my fingers across the dainty lace throw at the end of the bed. Rathe stood in the doorway, not knowing whether to come or go. Instead, he scratched his head and stared at the floor.

"I like it," I assured him.

He gathered my words to be an invitation and stepped inside the room. "My nan made it." He nodded to the throw I had been touching.

"It's real pretty. I like it, too, but I meant the house." I couldn't hold back my smile. "I love the house...almost as much as I love you."

"Oh." He fidgeted beside the bed. "Thank you."

Feeling awkward and nervous, Rathe and I found ourselves downstairs, eating the pecan pie Aunt Virgie had made special for our big day. The kitchen table was just large enough for both of us. Again, it was perfect.

"Thank you," I said between the sticky, sweet bites.

"For what?"

I shrugged. "For seeing something about me no one else can. I know you built this house for Bethanne, and I'm certainly no Bethanne."

"I'd never wish you to be someone else."

Resting my fork on the side of my empty plate, I sat back and looked him in the eyes. "I know. That's why I agreed to marry you. That's why I have love in my heart for you."

"I don't want you spending our entire life thinking that..."

"Oh, I won't. There isn't nothing of Bethanne here but the memory of what could have been, and those types of memories fade because they weren't meant to be in the first place. I look around, and I see you. Everywhere. Your love built an old house up from the grips of oblivion. It would never exist right now without you being in this world. And it's a lovely house, but you weren't able to make it a home on your own. I'm here now. Our love will make it a home." My eyes scanned the kitchen, imagining where I would hang flowers to dry, or place the sugar dish Momma gave me as a wedding gift, passed down from her momma.

Nodding, so happy I was practically laughing, I whispered, "I'm home."

I was starting to see where Preacher Smith was going with his baby feet sermon. Rathe and I were going to build a home inside of this house. We were the bones that everything would rest on. Something flashed in his eyes, and I knew he saw it, too.

Rathe's fork clanked as it dropped onto the empty plate.

I thought he was getting ready to leave the table, and he sort of did.

He slunk to the floor at my feet, removing my slip-on shoes. I shook my head, warning, "They're dirty," as I tried to pull my feet free. The only time I put my shoes on all day was to hop in the wagon because I didn't fancy stepping on nothing in the dark when we arrived, not knowing the land well enough yet.

Holding my feet in the gentlest manner, he said, "Then I'll kiss the dirt you walk on." And true to his word, he laid those lips right on the bottom of my foot in a way that made me blush brighter than a single raspberry left on the bush.

"I'll always kiss your feet," he promised, "because I always want them walking home to me." A finger traced my leg all the way up until it connected with my right hand. He pulled it into his, turning my palm up to Heaven. "I'll always kiss your hands." The soft press of his warm lips on the middle of my palm sped my heart. "Because these hands will hold our babies when they cry and rub the dirt from my brow when I can't do it myself."

I beamed. We first met last year while he was helping Daddy with the tobacco. There was dirt across his whole face and his hands were full. I feared the sweat would run the mess right into his stormy blue eyes that managed to sparkle even through the depths of shadows. Inhaling a breath, I asked him to close his eyelids and brushed it away with my bare hands. When his eyes opened, it was as if he saw more than a girl in front of him.

In our kitchen, Rathe rose to his knees.

He was so tall and I was the complete opposite that, while I was sitting down, we were rendered equal. He slid his hand through my straw-colored hair until it rested on the back of my head, then he pulled me to him. "And I'll always kiss your lips." Our lips touched, and I swore by God that I could feel those buildings I had studied for so many years crash down around us in a chaos to end everything I held true.

This life was mine, and the man before me was nothing like I'd ever known.

When he pulled away, he whispered, "Because I want to make you smile when the rest of the world can't."

Our dirty plates sat right on that table all night.

CHAPTER THREE

Creatures of Flight
1918

The following winter was, for lack of a better word, magical. Rathe and I worked hard during the punishing, cold days, and loved each other tight when the sun set. And we dreamed of what our little house could be some day. It was in our plans to turn the homestead into a farm. We had horses, but I envisioned cows and pigs and chickens running all which way across the property.

"We'll need to build a coop for the chickens and a lean-to for cows. Horse field's big enough to share. Might have to hold off on pigs, though."

"The barn's big enough for a few pigs," I reminded him.

Lying in the crook of Rathe's arm, the sun shining across our bed, I didn't know where my dream ended and his began.

"Yeah," he agreed, "but we gotta get enough wood for a pen, first, unless we buy pigs and wait on cows."

"Either way, we don't want to get more than we can feed." I sighed and rolled over to face him, my hand gliding across his bare chest. "I know it's going to take a long time to make this happen. I'm not expecting to peek out the window tomorrow and see a working farm. It takes sweat and muscle to make something happen."

He kissed my cheek. "You're about as smart as your daddy."

Blanching, I closed my eyes, but my mouth kept running. "Don't ever say that in front of my daddy, or he'll fire you and then we'll have nothing."

I tried to laugh, but Rathe hugged me tighter.

"Why is your daddy so hard on you?"

"'Cause I'm stubborn like he is, but I'm a creature made of different things."

He shook his head, agreeing. "You sure are."

The inflection in his voice made me think he was more than happy about that. He had a way of wiping clean something that made me feel bad and replacing it with something I couldn't help but feel good about.

Scanning the room, the way I always did to make sure it was all still real, my gaze fell upon a little box on the dresser. Rathe had never mentioned what was in it, and although he hadn't ever told me *not* to open it, I couldn't take it upon myself to be so bold.

"If I ask you something, will you answer?"

"Anything."

"What's in that box, there?"

He didn't even have to look to know just what I was speaking of.

"My daddy's corn pipe."

I wanted to lay eyes on it, but Rathe's tone made me feel like I oughtn't.

"Was he a good man when you were in his house, or was he hard?"

"Well... That ain't easy to answer. A man can be hard on you, but still be good. It's how you grow up. I grew up working. Never stopping for nothing like illness or celebrations. My folks worked harder than most. Probably why their burst of life was so short. So it depends on your definition, I reckon."

The way he spoke made them sound dead and gone. Then again, there are a lot of people who aren't quite living even though they're laboring hard to live.

Crossing my arms above the blankets, feeling the release of air through the feather comforter, I said, "Using your definition, what kind of man was your daddy?"

"A little bit of a lot of things. Just like my momma."

I smiled at that. "I guess we're all a little bit of a lot of things."

"No." He looked into my eyes. "Your daddy was right. You're mostly trouble." Laughing, he wrapped me into his arms.

I pretended to fight for a second, but I wasn't able to keep up the ruse. Snuggling my head on his chest had become my favorite shame in life.

The covers, piled high, gave us the illusion of being in a warm bubble. I moved my foot back and forth, enjoying the feel of the blankets across my toes. The moment could catch, and I'd never have a problem staying right where I was, eyes closed, just swaying my feet, feeling the pull of joy. Soon, Rathe found my leg with his, and we shared a mischievous smile.

It was Sunday. We should have been in church.

Which was why I was more than a little shocked to hear my momma's voice call from outside as the front door rattled under the pounding of her fists.

"Nora May Cravis, don't you make us wait in the cold! You open this door right now!"

Our eyes about popped out of our heads.

"Holy hell, is that your momma?" Rathe was already out of bed and had his pants halfway up his legs by the time he finished saying his own question.

I rushed to my feet and threw on the thin cotton dress draped over the chair by my side of the bed. Running down the stairs barefoot, I stopped to compose myself and brush my hair down with my hands before opening the door. Oh, how I'd have given anything not to have to open that door and look my momma in the face.

"Hi, Momma," I said calmly. Holding the door open wider, I asked, "Would you like to come in?"

"Would I like to come in?" she balked. "I certainly didn't traipse all the way out here, dragging your sister and cousin along, just to stand on your porch, staring at that mangy, cross-eyed dog of yours. So yes, we would surely like to come in."

"His name is Toes," I reminded her softly. "And he ain't mine. He just likes to sit there sometimes."

Toes was a wanderer. Straw could replace his fur and it wouldn't make it any harder. The only thing about him that was cuddly or fluffy happened to be his toes. But his nails were uneven on account of all the wandering he did, so I stuck to patting his head anytime he stopped in.

Momma stomped past me into the house, giving me a sideways glare something awful. Shailene and I shared a quick smile once she had her back to us. We always found Momma funniest when she was incensed.

"I don't find anything funny about it," Cousin Eula said as she passed us in the doorway. "I would think you're above such childishness now, being a married woman."

Cousin Eula had flaxen hair that resembled the old broom Momma kept around to sweep mud off the porch ever since I could remember. Her face was full and flush, though, and her round eyes called out like a siren's beacon to any boy in her immediate area. She was a full year older than me. How I married before she had would forever mystify us both. It was done, however, and she would never forgive me for it.

We converged in the kitchen as Rathe hurried past us to the back door.

"Hello, Rathe," Momma greeted. Sopping with false concern, she asked, "Has your household fallen ill? Has there been an emergency of the highest magnitude to garner staying home rather than gathering with your fellow men for morning worship?"

Frozen mid-step, Rathe stared at her for the longest minute in God's history before choosing to answer. I knew for sure he was thinking of the most brilliant excuse that would not only make Momma eat her words, but leave her so embarrassed as to never attempt such a spectacle again. Because, although I would always be her daughter, I *was* someone's wife now. And this was *our* home.

Rathe let go of the back door handle and faced us.

I smiled, waiting for his answer.

"Well, ma'am," he began, "nothing comes to mind. See you at dinner, Nora." That man had the audacity to shoot out the door like a jackrabbit. And when I turned to watch him run across the yard like the chicken he was, he turned, raised his hands as if in prayer, and mouthed the words, "I'm sorry."

The smile across his soft lips said otherwise.

Guess I couldn't blame him. No one wanted to be in a room with my momma when she was angry. Still, that man would be eating mud pies for dinner.

Turning to face my momma, sister, and cousin, I offered

them a slice of raisin bread and coffee, ignoring the itchy feeling of abandonment.

Momma shook her head, disapproving.

Shailene, having spent a lot of time in my little kitchen, knew right where the sugar dish was tucked away and set it on the counter.

"Thanks, Sissy."

She smiled in return and reached for the coffee cups, which had been a gift from Aunt Virgie. Understanding the healing power of a cup of coffee or tea, she thought it was quite an important gift for a new marriage, as there were sure to be times when we would need every bit of healing we could get. My aunt was a smart woman. If only she could have foresaw those times so I could have prepared more for them.

And there were times...

The smell of coffee filled the small space, wrapping us in comfort.

Momma sat down in one of the only two chairs and cleared her throat. "Nora, I would understand your actions if, perhaps, you were pregnant or, God forbid, sickly. Looking at you now, you sure as gall don't look sickly. And you're as skinny as ever, so I'm hesitant to believe you are with child. Am I right, or do you have news?"

Everyone was looking at me, mostly hopeful. Although Cousin Eula's jaw was locked shut, her brain battling her heart. She loved me enough to be happy if that were the case but allowed jealousy to run rampant enough to secretly plead for a different outcome.

Finally, I shook my head. "No, Momma. It's just me here, standing in my kitchen."

My sister's attention fell to the delicate hem of her dress

as Cousin Eula released a loud breath I hadn't realized she was holding in.

Momma held her head high. "Well, that don't mean nothing. You haven't been married but a few months. It took almost a full two years before your brother, Able, was gifted to us." Her brow crinkled. "You don't know how often I was gripped by fear before he came along. I had begun to think it wasn't a possibility." Pulling herself from old, haunting thoughts, she laughed. "My fears didn't hold water. I ended up with five strong children. They came in time. Yours will, too."

There were times like this when she tossed aside her notions that a mother should be only stern and resilient, and spoke to us like regular people. I loved these moments, far and few. I felt as though I was seeing Momma on a clear day rather than fighting through a thick fog of her making.

"I want ten children!" Shailene proclaimed, interrupting the moment with her unique enthusiasm.

Momma laughed a hardy laugh. "I believe you, girl."

"How many do you want, Nora?" Cousin Eula asked. "I only want three. I have no intentions of being a farmer's wife. I want to live in a city. A big one."

"I believe that, too," Momma interjected.

The hopeful thought that everyone would forget that I hadn't answered her question fled when they fell silent and stared, waiting for me to join the conversation.

I shrugged. "I don't know. I don't spend much time thinking about it, I guess."

"You don't think about it?" Cousin Eula spat. Her hair clung to her head like a bristle brush as she continued. "You're married. You've got a sturdy home. Why wouldn't you be thinking about it?"

Again, everyone turned, waiting for my answer.

Looking directly at my mother, I said, "I don't know," and poured coffee in the white cups gathered on the counter.

The airy feel was immediately swept out of the room.

Momma frowned, her lips resting in a straight line. "What *do* you know, Nora?"

And just like that, the fog was back, and I was lost in its midst, prey for her antipathy.

"Do you know how hard it is to be grown, with grown problems? Do you know what a true hard day's work feels like? Do you see all that your husband does for you?"

I began to shrug, but she only got louder and angrier.

"Don't you dare! Don't you dare shrug or tell me, 'I don't know, Momma.' I don't want to hear it anymore." She set her coffee down and stood. "Those are little girl vices, and you're standing in front of me, a woman. Act like it!"

My heart jolted, like little men pounding from the inside out with iron tools.

"Act like it?" I asked, not even realizing the words were readying to fly out of my mouth. I moved to stand straight rather than lean against the counter. "You're gonna march over to my house at this time in the morning, demand that I get out of my bed with my husband, and be accountable to *you* for my choices?"

Something was prowling inside me. It was another version of me that had never felt the need to climb to the surface and be seen before. I wasn't sure I appreciated it or not, for this was assuredly a defining moment in our relationship.

"You're right, Momma. I'm not a little girl anymore. I never wasted my words on your anger before because it wasn't worth the air that I needed to say them. That's my fault for feeling that way. But now I feel differently."

"Oh, you do, do you?" she practically yelled.

My voice was even and calm, but there was a hardness to my person that was new. Again, I wasn't sure I should fear it or feed it pride.

Cousin Eula and Shailene remained as silent as the dead. They were smarter than I was.

"If I want a hundred children or none at all, that's for me and Rathe to decide. Not you, Momma. And if I choose to spend the morning in bed, naked with my equally naked husband, that's for me to decide. Not you. Momma, you are always welcome in my home, except today." I picked up everyone's coffee cups and set them in the sink. Turning to face them, I gripped the sink behind my back.

They looked stunned, each of them. Shailene just couldn't believe that I said the word "naked" in front of our mother in context to a man. Cousin Eula, it was clear, couldn't wait to spread the depths of my mental and emotional thickness to the rest of the family. And Momma... Well, she didn't know whether to blush or let the steam billow from her ears.

Her voice deflated and she muttered, "My own daughter. Next you'll be fighting alongside those insufferable women outside the White House. You already conduct yourself more like a man than a woman. Why not vote like one."

Aghast, I stood my ground. "Maybe I will, Momma. I'll take my place right next to Daddy, Able, James, and Dewey. I know my place." Tears burned the rims of my eyes, yet I held them back with the fierceness of the rising sun. "Do you know yours? Or do you just do what you're told?"

"Come," was all she said.

The two girls followed behind, but not before Shailene snuck a quick hug.

I whispered in her ear, "Momma will let you come over tomorrow afternoon. Give it till morning to ask her." Then I kissed her on the top of her silky head and watched them leave.

Without turning to face me, Momma yelled, "I expect to see you at Miss Cecile's house Wednesday evening for weekly prayer, Nora May Cravis! If you can get your tail out of bed!"

Unsure how to accept the feelings that had come over me in a wave of fire, I decided to think on them. Not rushing to apologize and not rushing to gloat.

That evening, Rathe slunk back in. He took his boots off without me having to ask. But I stayed true to my word. Almost.

Sneaking from behind, he wrapped his arms around my waist and pulled my back to rest against his chest.

Setting the dishes down, I said, "I wish you would have come home sooner to give me time to pluck your feathers before dinner."

"I know, I'm nothing more than a chicken."

I could hear the smile in his tone without having to turn around and see it.

Fighting the humor in my own tone, I informed him, "Smile all you want, but you're having two-day-old stew for supper."

"Rightfully earned," was all he commented before kissing my neck. "How was the rest of your visit?"

Thinking for a minute, I finally settled on, "Informative."

Rathe pulled me around gently to face him. "Are you... Are you happy here?"

"Why would you even ask that?" I wouldn't have been more stunned if he had grown bumblebee's wings.

"I know you try hard to do and be. You've said as much in the past. But I know, deep down," he tapped on my chest, "there's a wildness in there that don't like cleaning dishes, don't like being and doing all the time."

Standing together in the warm kitchen, smelling of overcooked beef and vegetables, I gave his concern due thought before answering, "Sometimes."

"We're here to make our own futures, not to repeat those of the people around us."

Rathe hugged me tighter than I'd ever been held. Grabbing my hand suddenly, he yelled, "Come on!"

"Where?"

Smiling so big and bright, he nodded. "Out there."

We ran outside into winter's night, hand in hand, into the darkness of the hillside. We ran for a small eternity, only stopping when our ears were frozen, our hearts satiated.

Giggling, I leaned into him. "We're going to freeze to death out here."

"Or maybe we're going to live." Rathe snuck a peck on my lips.

Before he could snag me into an embrace, I took off running as fast as my legs would carry me, yelling, "Come with me!"

And he did.

Our hearts ran together many a night, across the fields as well as in each other's arms. We also found a balance, strained at times, with my momma and the rest of the family.

Shailene spent a lot of time with us, offering company when I had to run errands, like delivering grains to Cannady Mill Dam Gristmill. Secretly, we enjoyed the day, fishing a bit and, depending on the season, snacking on blackberries, figs, apples, and persimmons. And her green thumb saved our garden on more than one occasion. Without her, I do believe the vegetables would have uprooted themselves and marched clear out of sight to escape my efforts. I wished on many a star that Shailene could move in. Momma, however, said it wouldn't do. Shailene was about to turn fourteen and needed the benefits of being around strong, proper women. Apparently, I was not one of such women. Though, if we timed it perfectly and Momma was in a good mood, she would often allow Shailene to spend the night.

By our second Christmas, Rathe and I had finished an oak lean-to in the back field, complete with two cows. It was nice not having to go to Momma's for butter. As spring approached, some of my fondest memories were the afternoons when Shailene and I milked the cows, or the mornings when we sat in my kitchen, taking turns churning the sweet milk. The lean-to, however, proved to be a crucial hiding place from the rest of the world, where we shared laughter and secrets. Anything could be discussed away from sensitive ears.

"This is beautiful. How'd you make it?" I asked one afternoon, holding Shailene's hairclip cut from white material in the shape of a graceful bird.

She took it from my hand and smiled with satisfaction. "Do you really like it?"

"I wouldn't lie."

Clipping it into her hair, she said, "Making things just comes easy to me. I sewed around the edges and attached it to an old, ugly clip I wasn't using. The material was scrap from Cousin Adelaide."

"Well, it suits you."

"I love birds," she reflected. "If we were birds together, we could fly across land and sea. We could perch on top of those tall, fancy buildings you love from Aunt Virgie's pictures. I wish I could be a bird more than anything sometimes."

"Really? I think they're pretty, but I find them kind of dirty and unruly."

"See, you already have something in common with them!" Shailene joked. Laughing, she added, "You overthink things."

"Rathe would agree with you, there. That's one of the things I love about him, though. He speaks his mind. That's healthier than holding it in, you know."

A seriousness washed over Shailene. Hunched over the pail of fresh milk, she stared for a moment, listless. There was an unusual weight to her thoughts. As she took a deep breath and rubbed the edge of her faded navy dress, she unleashed a bit of them onto me.

"Sissy, how'd you know that you loved Rathe? In the beginning, I mean."

The day was blossoming into a gorgeous sight. A light scent of honeysuckle and onion infused the breeze.

"I guess I didn't. Not at first. There was something different about him. I remember wanting to find reasons to visit the fields while Daddy and the boys were out there working."

Shailene pushed her hair back. It had grown immensely long, and she refused to cut it, though the chore to brush it usually fell on me.

"So it was spending time together?"

"Partly. Loving someone is a confrontation of many things. And I think those things change from person to person."

I looked up from the udder and saw the blank expression on Shailene's face.

Taking a moment to stretch my back and legs, I couldn't help but ask, "Is this about Widow Baker's boy, Jonathan?"

"No!" Shailene's lip turned upward slightly into her embarrassed grin. "Definitely not."

"Just checking." I smiled.

Resolutely, she asked, "Go on. What were you going to say?"

"For me," I continued, "Rathe lets me be. I try my best to do what needs to be done, and he loves me regardless of the things that don't get done. We all know I won't be like Momma or Aunt Virgie, or even Cousin Eula. I can only be me. Rathe encourages that, and that's pretty special. I do the same for him in my own way. That's love, at least for us."

Shailene stared off into the field like she was daydreaming. I knew she was listening to every word, though. Our parents would have reprimanded her for being rude, but I left her alone. It takes a lot of time to process something like love. It doesn't happen in one conversation, let alone an afternoon. Or a lifetime, in some cases.

"What are you thinking, Sissy?" I asked her.

"Just wondering if I've felt real love."

"Have you?"

"I can't say yes... I can't say no, either."

In hindsight, I should have listened more closely.

I should have known something wasn't right.

CHAPTER FOUR

In No Uncertain Terms
1920

The summer of my twentieth birthday marked a clear change in how I viewed the world, how I invited it into my heart. This was the summer my sweet Shailene disappeared. She was no more than fifteen. Her cheeks were still round as pie with youth.

After our perfect summer milking and making butter, Shailene stopped coming around as often. It should have concerned me right away, but she was getting older, taking on more responsibilities at home with Momma and Daddy.

It made sense when they started pushing for her to get a job in a textile factory. Shailene's fair skin had always made it clear that a life of farming would be far harder on her than most.

One afternoon at Momma and Daddy's, while Momma and I had been trying real hard to mend our feelings, which called on more power than God needed to create the Garden of Eden, I found that other part of me, the one that often remained hidden far below the surface, undetectable, rise to defy Momma.

Shailene would never speak up for herself, and I could gather that she didn't prefer to work so far from her family.

"I'm agreeing with you, Momma, but I don't see why she has to move three towns over when there's work so close to home."

"It ain't about the work. It's about the experiences that come along with it," Momma pressed.

"Where was that belief when I was her age? I ain't been nowhere."

"And look how you turned out," Momma grumbled. "Least you could have brushed your hair before coming over."

Subconsciously, I rubbed my unkempt hair with my palm before I could stop myself, but answered, "You know I did."

I stood in their living room, staring at Shailene, who had become uncharacteristically despondent in the month following up to Momma and Daddy's decision.

Rubbing the sweat off my hands across my light dress, I attempted to capture her compassion. "Won't you miss stitching and reading the Bible together?"

Momma balked. "Of course. We both will."

Hearing our rising tones, Daddy stepped into the boiling living room. His once-white shirt was tan from red clay. His pants sagged, showing the effects the sweltering summer was having on his weight.

Dewey followed him into the room, just as threadbare as Daddy. However, Dewey's rosy skin and crafty eyes kept him from ever looking truly worn. He was over two years older than me, but he forever passed as my little brother, partly due to his pluck.

My eyes met Daddy's when he said, "We will all miss Shailene, but we're doing what's right. Except you. Would you like to clarify how running into our home and telling us we're wrong is acceptable?"

Oh, how I wanted to remind him that Momma had done exactly that to me and Rathe not so long ago. Speaking such a truth, however, came with severe consequences of which I was unprepared to face.

I took a moment to wipe the sweat from my forehead and neck.

My relationship with my father had become more strained, if that were ever possible, when Rathe took a job in Henderson, foregoing tobacco farming, when tobacco started dying from the Wilt. Daddy didn't think there was much stock in building school busses. He thought the whole of Eastern North Carolina had lost its ever-loving mind, thinking they needed vehicles for perfectly healthy children. "I walked mile upon mile for an education. If it's handed to you, won't nobody appreciate it," he insisted.

But hidden deep in his tone, I heard the fear. Because a lot of crops were being lost to the Wilt. A lot of farms were going bankrupt, and there was no name for the feeling of watching it happen, not being able to stop it, knowing your own family could be next.

Truth was, Daddy couldn't afford to keep Rathe. He and Momma struggled to maintain life with their tenant farmers. But if he admitted this to even himself, the fear might slither from his head right into his heart and turn it blacker than the dead rows of tobacco.

"I'm not trying to tell you anything different, Daddy. I wish she wasn't going so many miles, is all. I don't have any means to visit anyone so far."

"Shailene's future is not dependent on whether or not you are comfortable with it."

"I understand that, Daddy."

"Do you? You talk to one of your farm animals with more respect than you do to your own momma. And now you're here, in my house, trying it with me. With all of us."

He was trying to make me feel like I was a child again. Backing me down, like he used to. Only a nagging feeling that Shailene was being placed in a predicament kept me from folding to his will.

For fear that I would be thrown out after I said what I needed to say, I rose and stood in the doorway. Dewey sat across from Shailene, confused as usual. Daddy stood next to Momma's chair, hand on her shoulder. Shailene never made eye contact with me or anyone else. Not once.

"No one expects me to keep quiet," I mustered. "Don't expect me to be proper, either. And for that...I'm damn thankful."

Momma about fell out of her chair, hearing me cuss for the first time. Daddy went utterly still before he lunged to grab me.

Moving quicker than the angry man before me, I weaved through the living room, escaping his grasp, yelling, "I know when something's not right, and sending Shailene off like this ain't the answer." Taking a moment to look my momma in the eyes as I hopped over a sitting stool, I warned, "You do this and nothing will ever be right again, Momma. I feel it in my bones."

Daddy chased me right out of the house, belt in hand, ready to beat me like a child.

I started to run, but that hardness in my gut made me stop and turn to face him. "Do it," I dared. "I'm only a reflection of the man who raised me. Do it."

A peculiar look crossed my daddy's face. It was so foreign, I could have been looking right into the eyes of a stranger.

The belt dropped out of Daddy's hand into the long grass by his side. It was as if someone stole the fight right out of him.

"I can't do this anymore," he acknowledged.

"Do what?" I asked, not willing to step closer.

Momma and the others stood on the porch, mouths agape.

He shook his head. "Go. Go be grown. It's best if you leave the business of raising your sister up to us."

"Are you telling me to leave?"

He nodded.

Stepping closer, expression neutral, I asked, "For good?"

"Maybe." He was fidgeting, which was not in his usual nature.

"Because...I could be grown and still come to Sunday dinner."

Turning sideways, choosing to stare off into the field rather than face me or Momma, hands resting in fists on his sides, he nodded again. Clearing his throat, he conceded, "If your mother is all right with that, I believe you could be grown and still come to Sunday dinner." Looking straight at me, he warned, "But you cuss one more time and we'll wash your mouth out with soap. I don't care how grown you are."

"I can mind that."

Daddy picked up his belt and looped it through his pants as he walked up the front steps, past everyone else, and disappeared inside. I heard him say, "Ruth, I believe I'm gonna need that whisky now."

"It will only take a minute," Momma said. She wrestled for a moment with the thought of saying something to me. That was clear. In the end, however, she chose silence, though her hesitancy to walk inside seemed laced with remorse.

We both walked away that day from the judgments we harbored for one another.

Before Shailene followed her and Dewey in, she stepped off the porch, wriggling her bare toes in the grass.

"This is for you, Sissy." She held her closed fist out.

When I reached out in front of her, she dropped the dainty white bird-shaped hairclip into my open palm.

"I can't accept this," I said. "It's your favorite. It's too beautiful to waste on me."

"Please," was all she said.

"Okay." I wrapped her in my arms and kissed the top of her head, though she was almost as tall as me. Reluctant to let her go, I made myself. "Okay. I'll wish on a star for you, Sissy."

Shailene walked inside without another word or glance.

That walk home was the longest of my life. I didn't know whether to turn around and fight or accept what was out of my control. The inner conflict caused a numbness to wash over the important parts of my brain by the time I made it home. And a piece of that numbness, I suspect, slowly killed a valuable part of who I used to be.

Momma made a lot of excuses that year before my sister was, in some manner, erased from my life. Shailene always did prove to be the Eden of my memories until the day my body gave way to the graces of this good earth.

I spent many long days alone during this time, envisioning Shailene beside me, helping with whatever chore I was attempting. Her smile was clearer than my hands in front of me. We would talk for hours in my head.

Always, though, I found myself begging her to come back to me. A wash of tears would replace our laughter and reality would find me alone, staring into nothingness rather than working.

CHAPTER FIVE

Songbird

Possibly out of pure bewilderment, unable to cure my heartsickness, Rathe traded some of our canned goods and a bit of carpentry work for a special gift.

It was November, four months since Shailene had been sent off. Momma and Daddy had prepared for her to come home and visit over the holiday, but Sissy was unable to make it. There was an emergency order at the textile mill, and they needed girls to stay and work. Daddy mentioned what a tremendous opportunity it would be for her to prove how serious she was about her position with the company.

I was so angry with him for even suggesting she not come home that I refused to eat Thanksgiving dinner with him and Momma. Rathe and I ate stew with a fresh loaf of bread I'd made to take over to their house.

We ate in silence, and when I rose to place the dishes in the sink, Rathe snuck a gift from the other room and set it on the table. It was wrapped in plain white paper, the kind the mercantile used to wrap delicates in.

"What do I do with this?" I sat down at the table across from Rathe, confused.

"Some people try opening presents." He smiled and pushed it closer.

"I just wasn't expecting a gift of any sort. Are you trying to start a new tradition?"

"It just struck me as something you might be needing."

The parcel covered my entire lap as I pulled it to me. It was thin and wide.

"Be careful," he cautioned. "It's kinda fragile."

Tearing the paper into careful strips, a rich, wooden form began to peek out.

"I can already tell you, it's too fancy, whatever it might be."

Clearing away every last bit of paper, I was left holding the strangest instrument I'd set eyes on.

Knowing by my blank expression that I hadn't any idea what it might be, Rathe chuckled. "It's an autoharp." When I remained silent, he explained, "You play it."

Blinking and looking across the table, I confessed, "I don't know how. I can't imagine where to start."

"You'll learn."

"Where is this coming from? Is the after-dinner conversation becoming tiresome?"

"No."

He slunk to his knees in front of me. It brought back the memory of him on our wedding night, kneeling just like so. Only, this time we felt completely at ease to be so intimate with each other. It felt righter than the stars shining on a clear night.

"Nora, I know your heart aches for your sister, and there ain't nothing I can do about that. I can't bring her back. I can't send you there. There are too many *can'ts* in this calculation." He touched the autoharp still on my lap. "This is my way of recognizing your pain. Maybe you can get some of that happiness back. And I wouldn't mind hearing your voice paired with this equally delicate instrument. It would be a thing of angels."

Leaning forward, I rested my cheek on the top of his head.

"Thank you." I spoke low, feeling the vibration of my voice throughout his dark curls. "I don't know if that will ever happen or not but thank you for trying. For having faith in me. And for that, I promise to try, too."

I loved this man kneeling before me. I loved him more day by day. He made it so easy to want to do right by him.

So I tried.

As the days drew drastically shorter, the frost sneaking up on Mother Nature's bounty, I fed the animals, cared for our home, and took every spare minute to practice the auto-harp. It wasn't as difficult as I'd originally feared.

Momma had been a schoolteacher before she married Daddy. My brothers, Shailene, and I never went one day without practicing our vocabulary and spelling. And during special occasions, she was able to borrow a few instruments for us to learn on. Of course, nothing I had played was quite like the autoharp, but it wasn't all that different, either. There were strings. They needed tuning. Then they needed old-fashioned practice.

I got to where I could strum together some handsome notes, of which Toes was forever thankful for. His gratitude was apparent the day he stopped howling over my attempts.

In the evenings, after supper, Rathe would tend to the fire in the living room and then relax awhile, listening as I fulfilled my promise. Not only had I tried, but succeeded in finding a scrap of joy in the darkness that had cloaked my heart.

As Christmas came about, I even found it in my heart to

invite my family out for a fancy Christmas Eve dinner. Momma accepted right away, dragging my brothers and Cousin Eula along. Daddy came, as well, bringing cigars for the men to smoke on the front porch.

The only stab in my heart was knowing I wouldn't be setting a place at our makeshift wood table for Shailene. I tried, nonetheless, to open myself to the healing possibilities of family togetherness. Although, we were talking about *my* family.

Momma, Cousin Eula, and I worked shoulder to shoulder in the kitchen, preparing for a grand feast.

"I can't believe how fast Rathe was able to build a dining table to suit everyone. He is becoming quite the woodsmith," Momma complimented.

"Thank you, Momma. You should mention it to him. It would make him proud to hear such a compliment."

"I'll be sure to, Nora."

I wiped the sweat from my hairline, taking a moment to twist my hair up and pin it to the back of my head in a tight little bun. I hated to tie my hair back, but there were times, like cooking, when it was unavoidable if I didn't wish to serve it on a platter.

We took turns chopping and cutting, and Cousin Eula wasn't too pleased to be shucking the corn. She had practically married herself off already, though there wasn't a suitor lined up anywhere. We were all hoping the day would come sooner than later, God willing, before she drove us all crazy with her talk of high society and eleven-dollar dresses. I mean, who could afford to wear an eleven-dollar dress? Not when we had a mighty need to eat and feed the livestock!

"Can I set the table? My hands will be too raw to eat if I shuck anymore."

Momma fought back an exasperated grumble and cleared her throat instead. "Check the basket I set in the dining room. I brought enough linens and silverware to set a place for each of us."

She practically skipped out of the kitchen. Momma and I looked at each other and shared a smile.

It was nice...being like this with her. It was true, we had a lot of rough patches. A lot of miles walked side by side, but more lonesome than being on one's own. And it wasn't supposed to be like that, I knew in my bones.

"Thank you, Momma, for being here."

"Well, I wouldn't have it any other way, baby."

Cousin Eula finished setting the table. It looked beautiful adorned with all of Momma's tableware from her momma and her momma's family.

Daddy yelled from the porch, "How much longer are you gonna keep us waiting?"

"It'll be done shortly," Momma singsonged through the house.

While we stacked dishes and prepared the vegetables on limited table space, I dared ask what I had been wondering, not holding my tongue back.

"Will Shailene be coming after Christmas?"

Momma dropped the spoon in a bowl she was holding.

"Why?" Turning to confront me, she asked, "Why do you have to do this now?"

Looking down at the corn cobs in my hands, I muttered, "Because she's still a part of this family, and if we stop talking about her, it's like she's not." Motioning from her to me, I said, "How is this supposed to work, you and me, without Shailene? We need her so we can exist in the same world together, Momma."

"Your sister ain't gone for good. Stop acting like a lost child."

"How should I act, Momma?"

"Like anything but this! How will you be a mother if you can't even act like a grown woman?"

My breath caught. Momma knew that was a sensitive matter. Although I had all but forsaken the idea of children, I knew Rathe held out hope. It meant so much to him.

The family had begun to whisper a year ago. I caught the tail of hushed conversations when I entered a room sometimes. Other times, it was an unintentional look that told me all I needed to know they were thinking.

I endured the most from Momma. Not because of words or looks. Because she placed the cruel notion into my imagination like a trap that Rathe might seek out a woman who could give him the life that I couldn't. "Every man needs to feel eternal in his children," she once told me. My perspective was, "Love is love. An empty womb won't change the love Rathe and I have created together." All she said in return was, "Only time tells the truth."

And here we stood again, locked over the matter.

"What good will it do, Momma, to impose your belief on the matter when it don't fit?"

With her hands on her hips, Momma warned me, "Child, I've got years of wisdom on you."

"I ain't a child no more!"

"Oh," Cousin Eula belted as she flopped into a chair, "Here we go again!"

"Hush up!" I retorted.

"I will not have this!" Momma yelled. "Stop it."

"Why, because it's unfitting of a young lady? A future mother?" I started throwing corn cobs at the table before my words died.

Cousin Eula shook her head. "You're crazy. Here! Ruin the beans while you're at it!" She flipped a bowl over, spilling green beans all over the table and floor.

Momma gasped. "What's gotten into you, Eula Gene?" Snatching the bowl out of Cousin Eula's hands, she clanged a spoon against it, creating a loud, hollow noise to grab our attention.

Daddy walked in, flustered with hunger. "Is dinner ready yet?" he asked in a huff, quickly realizing that something was amiss.

We froze, scowling at one another. Momma grasped the bowl so tight her knuckles were turning white. Cousin Eula had green beans hanging from the side of her hand from where she had been smashing them on the table with her fist. And I stood in the middle of all the chaos, as usual, in a litter of corn cobs.

Clearing his throat and turning from the kitchen, he announced, "Take your time. We aren't that hungry."

Daddy knew when he was outmatched. Three angry women in a kitchen... Well, that was a fight he didn't want any part of. Didn't understand it. Didn't want to.

We turned our attention back among ourselves. The heat of the moment having been interrupted, we found ourselves looking nothing more than silly.

I caught a grin forming on one side of my mouth. It must have been contagious because Momma's lips started to upturn, whether she wanted them to or not.

Flustered, Eula charged, "You're just queer." She started to wipe the green beans off her hand, watching them fall to the floor. "I don't know where to begin to understand you."

"She might say the same of you," Momma pointed out.

I shrugged. "I don't expect us to be alike or think the same."

Sweeping the beans back into the bowl Momma handed back to her, Cousin Eula huffed, "Ain't that right!"

"That's enough." Momma collected the wayward corn cobs that had rolled across the floor.

Bowing to help pick them up, I stacked them back on the tray with her. Cousin Eula continued to round up the green beans. Once we were all done, everything got an extra good washing before being cooked.

Momma beamed when we packed the table full of all manners of vegetables, pies, and the Christmas roast.

"Look at that." She glowed. "It's perfect. Even a little to-do can't stop us from creating a fine meal."

Leaving our aprons in the kitchen and calling the men into the dining room, all eight of us sat down for a holiday prayer.

Rathe sat at one end and Daddy at the other. I opted to sit next to Dewey and Able. Cousin Eula sat between James and Momma across the table. And between the food, we had collected a cluster of holiday flowers to spruce up the room and complement the red accents in Momma's tablecloth.

We thought it best if Daddy said the Christmas prayer.

"Dear Lord, thank you for this day of rest with our loved ones. For allowing us this fine meal that would not have been otherwise possible without the dutiful hands of these women who care for us so well. Thank you for everyone we hold dear, near and far. And thank you, good Lord, for forgiving the complexities of the human heart long enough to ensure the food made it out of the kitchen on plates rather than in a broom pan." Looking up to meet our moderately stunned faces, he added, "Merry Christmas. Let's eat."

Rathe cracked a smile but did as he was told. Everyone

dug in, filling our plates with food and our hearts with a good memory.

Able was into his second helping of cranberries and potatoes when he mentioned how tasty everything was, thanking us profusely. "It's a dang good meal."

It wasn't until James pointed out, "The corn's a little gritty," that us women busted out laughing. Daddy just shook his head, refusing to acknowledge our behavior, though we knew deep down that he found it humorous, too.

After dinner, I asked everyone to gather round in the living room. We pulled the chairs in from the dining room so that everyone had a proper seat. While my brothers ate the last slices of pie, I excused myself and fetched my auto-harp. Sitting down between Momma and Rathe a minute later, I announced, "You might have gathered already that I don't have much of a knack for playing instruments, but I have recently discovered, thanks to Rathe, that I sure do enjoy it. So I hope the joy it brings me shines through and brings you some, too. Merry Christmas."

So many of the songs I had made up involved Shailene. Though, after the moment in the kitchen with Momma, I thought it might be a respite to us both instead if I chose a song about the falling snow and the moments we make with our loved ones, safe from the dangerous touch of Jack Frost.

Everyone seemed spellbound as I reached the second verse, humming and singing lightly about sharing these hardships our ancestors once withstood. Thriving and enduring, finding the will among the sleepy oak trees to forge a home and a life.

My song, along with the melodious voice of the auto-harp, made such an impact that I sang a few more. The evening turned out to be rich with love and companionship. It was definitely a Christmas to remember for all time.

I hugged everyone extra tight before they loaded into the carriage for the ride home through the winding countryside. There were two large farms and a few neighbors between our homes. The road was run and checked so often, however, there was no chance of potholes or other obstructions, unless a tree had fallen under the weight of ice from the last storm. Winters never got so cold so quick, but this year had been a doozy.

As if reading my mind, Dewey assured me, "If there's a fallen branch or tree, we'll have it out of Momma and Daddy's way in no time flat."

Smiling brightly, he kissed my cheek. "See you around, Sissy." He joined everyone in the carriage, and they were off into the night, wrapped snug in lap blankets and wool coats.

See you around, Sissy.

The smile never wavered from my lips, but Dewey's words threw me like a butterfly in a tornado. The boys hardly ever called me Sissy. Only Shailene used it often. For that instant, I so wished that it had been her voice speaking those words to me.

That night, Rathe and I wrapped our arms around each other tight, under the pile of blankets, and talked for hours.

It was the first time since Shailene had gone that I felt the urge to say little more than the necessary words to carry me through the day.

"I may not have an exceptional singing voice, but it fashions a connection between me and my family better than anything I've ever been able to say in the past. Thank you."

"Don't thank me. I wasn't the one singing for everybody. Believe me, if that were the case, they would have run out of here faster than you could sneeze."

His chest quaked with laughter, forcing my hand to move up and down, as it was wrapped over the top of him.

"Thank you," he breathed into my hair before kissing me.

"What have I done?"

"You're a magnificent creature. You must have been sent from the far-reaching light of a star. And you choose to be here with me, of all people on God's rock."

Unable to return such flattery, I kissed his lips as slowly as possible, trying to memorize every breath in this moment. That's how we fell asleep, tracing the tiniest of actions that build an overwhelming love.

But we woke up in the complete opposite manner, startled and shaken.

CHAPTER SIX

A Terrible Peace

ists slammed against our front door so hard the vibrations practically rocked the dishes right off the shelves. Rathe jumped up from a dead sleep, throwing his pants on and grabbing the Remington propped against the wall next to his side of the bed.

Rushing to the window, he threw it open and yelled, "Who's there?"

A young voice screamed up, frantic. "Baker! Widow Baker's son. Please help us!" His voice was ragged, as if someone had shredded his voice box. "Please help her!"

Rathe turned to me, and I ordered, "Go!"

He was down the stairs and gone before I blinked twice.

Throwing on a pair of riding pants and a long-sleeve blouse, I slipped on my boots and wrapped up tight in my thick coat. The Baker farm was a good ten minutes at a swift pace by horse. Hopping onto the back of our brown mare, I raced through the early morning. A thin mix of snow and ice crunched under hoof.

Upon turning the bend in the gravel road, I began to hear loud voices.

Almost there!

I rode up and dismounted to find Rathe holding his jaw, sitting on the ground next to an unconscious man. Widow Baker's son, Jonathan, the one who'd come to us for help, knelt next to a pile of cloth not ten feet away.

The Baker homestead was, in whole, a small cabin, two outbuildings, and a glorious red horse barn that would drive any man to envy.

"What is it? What's going on?" I demanded, waiting for anyone to answer.

Rathe looked tired, as though he'd aged twenty years since he left our bed. Wordlessly, he motioned with a nod in Jonathan's direction. There was something in Rathe's eyes, a reflection of a horror the likes we'd never witnessed.

Carefully, I walked up behind Jonathan, turning to look at his brothers, Colin and Daryl, standing on the steps to their front porch, lantern flames dancing by their bare feet. When they didn't blink, I looked down. The lantern didn't cut this far into the night, but I could see that Jonathan was holding his momma's limp hand. Under the pile of material was Widow Baker. Rather, a shell of what used to be.

"Oh, Jonathan... What happened?" I dropped to my shins next to him in the snow, placing my hand on his shoulder. The distinct smell of gunpowder interrupted the crisp air.

Jonathan was only sixteen. He reminded me of my own brother, Dewey, in so many ways, so it was twice as heart-breaking to see his eyes rimmed red from a thousand and one fallen tears.

"He came calling on her, said he had something impor-tant to ask of her." Closing his eyes, his head hanging low, I watched his dusty blond hair shift in the icy breeze. "We wanted to turn him away, but she refused to be that heart-less and agreed to hear him out." Trying not to get over-whelmed by tears, he wiped his face in the crook of his arm. "He was drunk. Had no business being here like that!"

"What happened then?" I asked quietly.

"He shot her in the neck."

Jonathan held his hand up in the dull light of the lantern, and I saw that it was covered in his momma's fresh, dark blood like someone had painted it on.

"She didn't say no. Why'd he do it? She didn't say no."

"He was asking for her hand? Like this?"

Jonathan nodded, wiping his face again. "Never even waited for her to answer."

I looked back at Rathe. He was no longer holding his jaw, but I could see him wrestling with an inner demon. The man beside him wasn't dead. Not yet. A peculiar gleam in his eye told me that he was thinking of doing the deed himself. Actually, by the flicker in Daryl and Colin's eyes, it looked as though he'd have to get in line and hope there was something left.

"The last thing she told us was to get back in bed, that she loved us."

I quickly turned my attention back to poor Jonathan on the ground. "She sure did love every one of you boys. And I know you love her just as dear, so let's get her off the dirty ground. Daryl, can you bring us a blanket, please?"

Honestly, I was looking to distract them. They had blood on their minds, and I didn't fancy watching that stranger die, as much as he might have deserved it.

Daryl nodded and walked inside. His gait was taut and slow.

Jonathan kept staring at his momma's bloodied face, praying that her eyes would open, that the pieces of flesh and smaller bits littering the snow would unaccountably fill the void in her neck. He was praying for a pure miracle.

Colin took it upon himself to bring out another oil lamp just about the time Daryl walked outside and down the porch steps with a thick wool blanket in hand.

"Thank you." I took the blanket.

I prompted Jonathan to help me lay it out smooth next to Widow Baker. That's as far as Jonathan made it. His bones locked up, and he collapsed to the ground.

"Jonathan," Colin started to chastise.

"No." I held up my hand. "He's fine. Why don't you and Daryl go get some shoes on?"

As if embarrassed for not having already done so, they headed in, but appeared a moment later, lacing their shoes on the porch.

I took it in stride, lifting Widow Baker's shoulders, cradling her wobbly head in the crook of my elbows. Shifting to the left, I set her down gently on the stretched-out blanket before setting out to lift her legs. Jonathan moved to help, but I motioned for him to stay where he was.

"We're fine," I assured him.

Once I positioned her right on top of the blanket, I made sure to straighten out her dress so she looked less disheveled and a little more like herself.

The stranger on the ground began to shift and grumble. It was obvious that one of the men had knocked him out right before I arrived. I was betting it was Rathe.

The men, all except Jonathan, rushed over and snatched the man from the ground.

Rathe said, "Wait a minute," and turned to me with an unspoken question. He was silently asking whether it'd be right to let them do with the man what they wished or whether we needed to fetch the law.

They all fell quiet, waiting on my decision. Not that they would abide by my wishes if they didn't see it fitting.

I shrugged. "I guess he left his fate in your hands when he came and did what he did." To Colin and Daryl, I said, "Do what you wish. We'll respect it."

They looked at Rathe for confirmation. He nodded and handed the man over to Widow Baker's sons.

"Do you know who he is?" I asked.

"Raymond Colt," Colin answered. "Lives out on the edge of the county."

"To the north," Daryl added.

Rathe shook his head. "Wait, don't Raymond Colt have a wife? That gal from Monterrey?"

"Ain't made an honest woman out of her." Colin spit on the man. "What made him think he was good enough for our momma? Man's nothing but a drunk, cavorting in speakeasies all damn night."

My husband shrugged. "Man like that... Don't know what all goes through his mind." His eyes swept over Widow Baker one last time as he said, "I'm damn sorry."

Colin always had a mouth on him, but that was one of the few times I'd ever heard Rathe curse.

He walked over to me and Jonathan. "Is there anything I can do here?"

"No. Go on home. I'm gonna stay awhile."

Raising my hand to his lips, his kiss lingered before he sighed. "I'll see you back at home."

I smiled, though it wasn't heartfelt. How could I feel even a fraction of real joy from his attention when Jonathan's momma was growing colder by the second?

Rathe rode home.

"What should we do?" Daryl asked.

It was my turn to make the decisions. Death was women's business. Men had their functions in it, don't get me wrong, but it was us women who tended to the dead. We gave them the last little bit of love their bodies would ever know again. We bathed them, took care in what they'd wear for the last time, made them look more like themselves. There's a truth in these actions that surpass prejudice like color or money. It's love. We take care of them in their last earthly happenings like our mommas would want someone to care for us. We offer a piece of our love to carry them over, wherever that may be.

"Colin, it would be a good idea to fetch the doctor." As he started to walk toward their horse barn, I added, "And Dorthea Daily. Your momma loved listening to her stories. I think she would appreciate one more."

I also had it on good authority that Widow Baker had thought Dorthea would make a solid match with her son, Colin, who was often too hardworking to pick his head up and look around once in a while. I didn't mind helping Widow Baker one last time. After all, these boys were on their own. They needed someone. Not to take care of them, but just to love them like the world would end if they didn't.

"Dorthea Daily?" Colin grumbled curiously.

"Yes. Don't be shy about it, neither. If you ask, she'll come. She loved your momma."

He didn't question me further. Daryl, however, was beginning to crack. I could see the wear of the night's events taking hold.

"Daryl, go to the mercantile and buy four yards of the best material they got. We're gonna make sure your momma has the best dress in Granville County."

"It's early, yet. They're not open." His voice sounded hollow.

"It will be by the time you get there. If not, they'll make an exception. Can you do that for me, Daryl?"

Pulling himself back from the numbness eating away at his soul, he nodded. "I can."

I smiled at him. "I know you can. That's why I asked you special."

He and Colin disappeared into the horse barn to saddle up.

As I covered Widow Baker with the blanket, wrapping from the left and right around her slack form, Jonathan began to cry again.

"How could this happen? Why would God take her from us? It's been less than a year since we lost our pa. We can't lose her, too." He looked up at me, tears streaking down his cheeks. "We can't."

"Oh, Jonathan..." I slunk down to sit on the cold, damp earth beside him. "I don't know why things happen the way they do."

"Isn't God supposed to protect us from this? My one fear was losing my momma, and God let that happen. He let her leave the house. He let Raymond Colt, drunker than a dunked rat, shoot her."

I wrapped my arm around him as he cried into the neck of my coat. We were about the same size, even though he was four years younger than me.

"I don't think God's supposed to stop people from being people, Jonathan. He can't make wishes come true. If that were the case, there would be too many wishes and not enough honest living." Hugging him tighter, I asked, "What would happen if you wished for the sky to be red and I wished for it to be purple? Is God supposed to choose you over me or me over you? That's not for a god to decide. He can only be here to help us make sense of the things we experience, not paint it like the picture we want to see."

Wiping his nose on his sleeve, he nodded.

"And I'd say you've been pretty lucky so far. Your momma was one of the very best I've ever known. And your daddy built this farmstead with his bare hands for you and your brothers, so that you'd have something worthwhile to gauge your dreams on."

"Yeah, I guess. But I don't feel so lucky right now." His voice quivered.

I fought back the quiver in my own. "I know." After a solid moment of nothing, I urged, "Come on, we gotta get you off the ground now."

He shook his head. "I can't."

"You have to." I stood and reached my hand down for his. "The lamps are drying up and we need to move your momma."

After a moment of consideration, he took my hand. I tugged him to his feet, and right into my arms for the largest hug I'd ever given anyone. When I pulled away, I smiled as I pushed his wild hair behind his ears. "Good job." And I meant it. We may have been the same size, but he was stronger than me. I didn't know what I would have done if he had refused.

Taking a moment to gather himself, he wiped his face one last time. "Let's get Momma out of the cold."

"The blood has slowed down, but there's still quite a bit. Should we move her to the barn instead of taking her inside?"

"No, my momma ain't going in no horse barn. Let's take her inside. We won't mind the mess."

"Okay." I was almost ashamed that I'd even suggested such a thing. I think Jonathan knew I meant well, though, so we let the topic lie.

Once we cleared their dining table and fashioned her in a comfortable position, we found ourselves sitting on the porch. Didn't make no sense because it was freezing outside, and we had been nearly solid ourselves when we brought her in. However, if given the choice to sit inside, staring at Jonathan's dead momma, or freezing our behinds off outside, we'd freeze.

The sun was pushing through the thickness of night, making itself known. And as it rose, the color washed from the world. Our skin looked pale, blending to the fabric around it.

Poor Jonathan looked like nothing more than a ghost himself.

"Thank you, Nora."

"You don't have to thank me."

He picked at the skin around his fingernails wearily. "And you didn't have to help us... Thank you."

"You're welcome, I guess."

It was a wait before Colin and Daryl returned. They had done what I asked of them. Dorthea was ever the lady, sitting behind Colin on his mount. Her curly honey hair had been swept into a thick braid, and she, too, chose a pair of riding pants. Though, she managed to embody a practical yet graceful presence while I could have believably been raised by coyotes.

Handing me the fabric, Daryl hopped down from his horse and suddenly wrapped me into his arms. I was enveloped by the musk of his sweat, able to hear his pounding heartbeat through layer upon layer of clothing.

Daryl wasn't much for saying thanks, but often showed it in other, if not awkward, ways. I appreciated the gesture.

"It'll be okay, Daryl."

"Daryl!" Colin yelled. "Release Mrs. Cravis before your stink sends her reeling and fetch a pale of warm water for Miss Daily, will you?"

Daryl and I looked at each other.

"You don't smell that bad," I said.

He cracked the barest of smiles but did as he was told.

Dorthea waved as she walked up the front steps. There was a moment of hesitation before entering the Baker home. I nodded encouragingly and the tension in her shoulders relaxed. Fortifying her nerve, she placed her hand on the back of Colin's arm and smiled. Colin appreciated the gesture, returning it with a courteous bow of his head.

I gathered my mare, Brownie, from the barn, loaded the fabric, and went home, leaving the Bakers to collect their shattered lives.

Rathe was working outside when I rode up.

"How is it over there?" He took the reins of my horse as I dismounted.

"Cold."

"What's that?"

"Cloth to make a proper dress for Widow Baker."

"You must be the sweetest soul." He kissed my forehead. "And tired."

I shrugged. "I don't have time to be tired."

"The dead got nothing but time. Rest awhile."

He walked the mare to the field, and I found myself sitting in our kitchen, rubbing the lovely cobalt fabric between my fingers.

It wouldn't make me feel better to rest when there was so much pain radiating through the hearts of our small community. So, I sewed. And when my eyes blurred, arms sagging, I recalled Widow Baker's laugh, and how she donated her time to anyone wanting, no matter the time or day. She was a jovial spirit, and we would all be a little less without her.

So, I sewed some more.

By Saturday, the day of the wake, it was finished. I rode it over to the Baker homestead. Dorthea met me at the door, and we took our time dressing Widow Baker in her Sunday best.

"This is a truly magnificent dress," Dorthea complimented. "The boys will be proud. Even now, like this, she inspires reverence."

"How are they doing?"

Dorthea was quiet for a time, thinking. "They need time," she settled on.

"I reckon so."

Widow Baker's wake came and went without incident. Her sons held up well. The entire community came out to say their farewells. It was a sight to behold.

The same couldn't be said for her funeral, for wildly varying reasons, though.

CHAPTER SEVEN

Wayward Smiles
1920-1921

It was half past four and everyone was gathered in the cemetery. Preacher Smith was his usual, long-winded self, talking about God's good grace and cherub wings.

Daddy was officially in a sleepwalk, Momma pinching his arm every two minutes to ensure he wouldn't fall flat on his face in the middle of the service. My brothers sat in back of the church. Rathe and I sat behind the Bakers and Dorthea in the first row, who held Colin's hand through every word Preacher Smith could think to say. In any other situation, I'm sure Colin would have been praying for it to never end.

As the service drew to a close, the church door opened, and everyone turned to see who had the audacity to show up at the end of a funeral.

A woman, at least in her late thirties, with hair as black as a nightly shadow walked in. As she pulled her shawl off and placed it on the back of a pew, the action exposed her rounded belly. The whispers gained momentum, sweeping from person to person, until the whole building buzzed.

Preacher Smith did his best to hush the crowd, finally securing a foothold. "Can we help you?" he asked.

The woman, her skin naturally tanned with the most subtle ruddy undertones, nodded in response.

"Well?" Preacher Smith goaded gently.

When she spoke with a rich accent, everyone shushed and leaned in as close as they could get without standing up.

"I came to pay respect to Mrs. Baker."

Preacher Smith asked, "Were you a friend?"

She held her stomach, as if it would support her rather than the other way around. "I am Luz Ravera. Raymond Colt was my fiancé."

A fluster rushed through the people of the church. I could hear my momma howl with shock, as did a few of the other women in attendance.

"Your fiancé?" Daryl questioned.

"For a short while, yes. We had been apart for many months."

Colin stood up. Dorthea wanted to pull him back down. That was plain. But that wasn't about to happen. Instead, he demanded answers.

"Raymond Colt was a drunk bastard who shot my momma in the neck. What business you got here?"

Again, shock coursed through the church. Colin was cursing in God's house. Although, I'm sure if there was any such a time to forgive a cursed word, it would be at your momma's funeral.

Luz's eyes welled with tears. "He was a desperate, greedy man. He suffered many vices. I come today to say how sorry I am that another woman befell his cruelty. Your mother would not have known him if not for me." Straightening her posture, she inhaled deeply. "Ramona Baker saved me from my own hand when I had no one. She has given me and my child a future. In return, we have taken hers." The tears ran freely over her pronounced cheekbones, falling to her cranberry-colored blouse. "I only wish to tell you, her sons, that I am sorry and lay my heart bare to ask your forgiveness."

No one spoke a word. Luz took this as a sign that she was unwelcome. She wrapped her shawl tightly around her robust form and turned to leave.

"Okay." Colin moved to stand in the aisle. Daryl and Jonathan broke their silence to ask what their brother was thinking. He raised his hand to silence them. To Luz, he said, "You ain't accountable for anyone's actions but your own. I forgive you."

Daryl agreed. "Momma wouldn't have it any other way." Standing to face Luz, he echoed Colin's sentiment. "I forgive you."

They waited for Jonathan to stand. He didn't. Not for a long while.

Just as everyone started to give up on Jonathan, he stood from the pew and approached Luz at the door.

"I'll never forgive my mother's death...but I don't fault you. I'd be wrong in doing so if that were the case." He found his coat on the hook and put it on, buttoning it shut. "I'd like to see you home safe, if that's acceptable."

Luz almost began to cry again.

"You are all the gentlemen she raised you to be. Thank you."

And just like that, Jonathan left his own momma's funeral to escort a stranger home. Some thought he was a little saint. Others, like my own momma, couldn't believe he'd walk a "questionable" woman home rather than stay and honor his momma. A foreigner, at that.

If you asked me, he was honoring his momma by being a decent person.

When they left, Preacher Smith tried to calm everyone. It was working, too, until one of the men in the middle row overstepped his bounds.

"What about Colt? Your momma's barely cold. Gonna forgive him as easily as you did that Mexican?"

The two brothers leapt over the pew so fast you would have thought they were sharing one brain. Colin snared the offending man by the collar of his shirt as Daryl reared back a fist, intending to hit him.

"Good Lord!" Momma squawked.

Everyone started shouting and scurrying about. Dorthea gasped, unable to do anything more. When I looked behind us, I could see the horror on Momma's expression. Unlike her, Daddy was purely amused, making no move to restrain the Bakers nor help the young man.

Rathe and I rushed to their defense when the crowd turned ugly on them.

"Get off them!" I shouted. "Their momma just died. Leave them alone!"

I stumbled backward when a hand reached out from the mob and pushed me. That's all Rathe needed. He reached into the fray and, pulling out an offending body, readied to punch him. Only, I hauled back and punched the man first, knocking him clean out of Rathe's grip. My husband and I shared a moment of authentic satisfaction.

"Stop it!" Preacher Smith yelled, "Please! Please, stop!" He waved his hands to garner attention. It weren't to be, though. Everyone involved had graduated well past rational thought.

The Bakers were beating the man something good. Unfortunately for the short, thick young man, Colin channeled every bit of conflict over his mother's death into the row at hand.

It wasn't until the man fell and they kept beating him that my daddy stepped in. Reaching his arm across Colin's torso, he looked him in the eyes. "That's enough, son. You made your point."

Colin's chest was rising and falling fast, like the ocean's tide, as he fought to catch his breath. To even his temper.

Dorthea couldn't have been more shaken by the evening's downward turn, but I gave her due credit. She hadn't run away. She waited patiently for Colin's senses to return and asked him to escort her outside. They were to ride together to his momma's gravesite, and she intended to do just that.

Daryl found me in the crowd, which was quickly dying down, and skewed his mouth, as if to say, "Whoopsie."

"Everyone," Preacher Smith announced, "it's time to head to the cemetery. Let's not make a second casket necessary by the time we arrive. We are all God fearing, after all." The good preacher was exasperated. Sweat laced his forehead. His knuckles were white from twisting a handkerchief in his hands. But he refused to lose control a second time.

The mood had turned weary by the time everyone exited the church. Rathe walked in front of me, my momma to my left. She was hanging on to my arm for dear life. Maybe to keep herself upright after such a fluster. Maybe to keep me from jumping in if trouble started again. Probably a little of both.

"My word, Nora," she muttered.

I braved the barest smile. "I think it's going well."

"You do, do you?" She shook her head. "And Hell's just humid."

Holding back a giggle, our eyes met. In all seriousness, I

asked, "Did you see how nice Widow Baker's dress turned out?"

There was something tired in Momma. Rather than fight, she nodded. "I sure did. Pretty as could be."

And by God, Widow Baker made it into the ground without further bedlam, and we all took to our homes quicker than birds fly south in winter.

I wish I had flown south, too. Just like Shailene wished so long ago. To fly free and high like birds.

Other than the excitement of Widow Baker's funeral, that winter felt empty. Quiet. Sometimes I visited the Bakers to break up the days, helping them learn the chores their momma used to tend. Even helping toss scalding water over every inch of their home for a week to rid them of an unprecedented case of bed mites after Daryl thought bathing wasn't of much importance anymore. We all learned otherwise and had a newfound respect for the sanctity of cleanliness.

When I was feeling really desperate, I'd travel on down the road and eat dinner with Momma, Daddy, and Dewey. James and Able had been courting two girls on their moonshine runs in the city. When they weren't working, they were in or on their way to Raleigh. Daddy was sure they'd defect to city life sooner or later. James swore otherwise. Able stayed silent on the matter. At twenty-four, he was ready for family life. Wanting it more than farming, that was for sure.

Either way, Daddy prepared himself for the news, whether it be what he wanted to hear or not.

When I wasn't in a state to be good company for anyone, I often walked the fields down the path from our house. I would steal a few hours and walk, just feeling the earth sway up and down under my feet, tripping over the occasional hoof indention. There was a settling power in the motion. And all the while, I would listen to the leaves create a melodious rhythm as the wind grazed each one. Nothing made me feel more earthbound.

People always talked about going to Heaven to live an eternal day of everything wonderful. Or to forget their lives and become one with the greater being. But those ideas scared me. What if some people are bound to the earth rather than the sky? I didn't want perfection and timeless beauty. I needed everlasting hope that the world would keep on changing, never ceasing to try harder and be better. What kind of place reaches a point where it stops trying? Where it don't have to try?

No, my soul needed something unexpected. Rain on a sunny day. A hard frost too early in the season. A hug when I deserved a tongue-lashing.

So I walked and walked, smelling the earth and listening to the wind speak, binding myself ever tighter to this green rock. Nothing healed my heart for Shailene, though. Momma scarcely answered my questions, vaguely offering that she was content working in the mill and was fine.

"I'll believe it when she's standing in front of me, telling me herself," I'd always answer.

Until the day came the following summer when she was, and she sure as all get-out did.

"Shailene!" I yelled, pulling up to Momma and Daddy's to see my baby sister sitting on the porch. My feet barely touched the steps as I ran to her, gathering her up into my arms as if she were the last light on the planet.

Crying, I could barely speak. At first, she was limp in my arms. I didn't care. I held on tighter. Slowly, almost awaking from a dream, her grip became stronger until it overpowered mine. We were locked in some sort of death grip and no one dared come between us.

Rathe and Momma stepped inside to give us some privacy.

"I didn't know you were coming home," I sobbed, rambling. "No one told me. I asked so many times and they never told me nothing real. Nothing."

"I'm here now," she whispered.

"Are you okay? Have you really been working in the textile mill?" Stretching her at arm's length to get a better look, I searched for anything telltale or out of sorts. Her cheeks were thinner, hair shorter.

Shailene shrugged. "It's the same me, Sissy."

"Yeah?" I smiled. Running my hands over her silky hair, I nodded. "Yeah."

"I'm back for good, Sissy."

I was so overjoyed I didn't even ask why. I could imagine. Shailene was too young for such a grownup way of life. She didn't have any business working in a big city. I was just thankful Momma and Daddy understood that now.

Momma ducked her head out the front door. "You girls hungry? We're eating in two minutes."

"Thank you, Momma." I almost laughed, I was so elated.

Rathe, Daddy, and Dewey were already waiting when we came in for lunch. A round birthday cake with one large candle sat in the middle of the table.

"Happy birthday, Nora," Momma said.

"Happy birthday!" everyone else shouted.

I couldn't believe it. Not only had they surprised me with a cake, but they had given me the best surprise of my life. My sister was home. That empty hole in my heart could heal now.

After blowing out my candle, I smiled at Rathe. The

relief was plain on his face. He had been holding his breath longer than he knew what to do with, wondering if I'd get back to being me. Now he had his answer. We were all smiling.

Rathe kissed my cheek. "Happy twenty-first birthday."

CHAPTER EIGHT

And I Heard A Man
1921

For the next month, I held true to being my old self. I visited Shailene every day, even taking along my autoharp. We sat together and sang for Momma as I showed Sissy how to play the instrument, too. With Rathe sometimes spending nights in Henderson during the week, I wasn't missed at home in the evenings. I had originally viewed it as a hardship, though, it turned into a blessing once Shailene returned, giving us due time to catch up.

There were moments when Momma had work that pulled her to other corners of the farm, which gave us a chance to talk in private. I had to admit, Shailene was a lot quieter than she used to be, but it was still her deep in that shell. I think the city was too overpowering for her. Country life spoke the language of her heart. That was for sure.

"Here." I held out my hand to her.

"What is it?" She reached for my hand.

"Just the most beautiful white bird I ever did see." I laughed and dropped the white bird hairclip into her palm.

"You kept it."

"Of course I kept it. It's too perfect to lose."

She clipped it in her hair and looked at me, seeking approval.

I nodded. "Exactly where it belongs."

From then on, she wore it every day.

It was almost like life before the city, only Shailene preferred to spend most of her time on the tobacco farm, at first, rather than explore or visit at my house. The only time she spent long periods away was when she went to school.

Momma thought it'd be good for her to spend time with her friends. Funny, since we never, none of us, spent much time in a schoolhouse. Momma was our schooling. She knew more than the teacher, banker, and preacher combined.

But I wasn't about to fight her over the decision. Shailene seemed to be enjoying it, and I was delighted to have her back.

It wasn't until the fourth Tuesday since Shailene's homecoming that everything unraveled. A fury had enveloped us, and we didn't even know it yet.

Packing up my autoharp, I had run back into the house to gather a few clippings of birds for Shailene out of the current *Country Life* magazine. One was of a red bird taking flight, wings outstretched. The other was of a perched hummingbird.

As I bounded down the porch, talking to Jonathan all the while, who had spent the afternoon picking blueberries with me, I saw a rider in the distance.

"That looks like your brother," Jonathan observed.

The horse hooves beat against the ground like a heartbeat, so hard I could feel it vibrating in my own chest. It almost felt as if I had two hearts instead of one.

I set everything down. "Why would my brother be coming here?"

James rode up in a thunderous cloud of dust. "Nora, something's happened."

He was my only sibling who refused to call me Sissy. Never had. It just never took.

"With Momma or Daddy?" I asked.

"Shailene."

"I don't understand."

An invisible heat poured over my skin. It crawled with anxiety to think of what he might say.

"She's gone."

I began to shake my head, fighting with my mind like it was molasses to make sense of my brother's words.

"But she only just got back," was all I could bring myself to reply.

Jonathan stepped up beside me and addressed my brother. "Can we help?"

"There's a search party down by the big creek, about a mile from the farm. We're going on four hours now."

"We're coming!" Jonathan shouted back as James galloped around the bend in the road and disappeared.

I left everything where it fell and leapt onto my brown mare, pulling Jonathan up behind me. It felt good to have him at my back. He had become the brother I'd so wished to have growing up. Dewey was a sweetheart, but he never paid attention for more than a minute without getting bored. Able was never around. And James never learned how to be softhearted.

Those first minutes of riding were painfully long. I put my mind on pause, not allowing it to think or panic or feel, because there would be no going back. For me, there would be no going back if my sister was hurt.

We helped the men in town search for hours, until the sun had well set long ago. I only stopped because it was unfair to ask Jonathan to do more. He wouldn't admit it, but he was worn thin. Able promised the search would continue if I left, so we went home.

I knew my daddy and brothers would bring Shailene back. I would have bet all the devil's men my own hide at that moment, I was so sure.

Rathe was away overnight in Henderson, as he was wont to do in the middle of the week. Jonathan slept on the living room sofa. We didn't yet have a spare bed in the second bedroom.

I smiled, thinking about what my mother would say if she knew Jonathan was sleeping in my house with Rathe away, working. I never took stock in gossip. Momma always worried that my actions would put into motion the wheels of the rumormonger machine. I always smiled and told her, "Toss in a penny and watch the show, Momma, because I can't change who I am."

Rathe knew full well the day Jonathan and I considered each other with romantic feelings would be the day God dressed up the world and called it a goat.

Jonathan was asleep before I could ask if he needed a second blanket. I set one down next to the couch just in case, smiling at his gawky feet sticking off the side of the couch.

Walking to the window, I stared into the night. It was so still. I could just as easily have been gazing at a lifeless painting. That's when the doubts started to set in, paralyzing and nauseating. Unsure as to whether I was talking to God or making a wish to my daddy, I found myself whispering, "Bring her back." To the world at large, I whispered, "She's not yours to keep. Don't take her twice."

As hard as I tried to calm my mind, I couldn't rest. The night was spent in half dreams, fighting with James and Momma one minute, screaming for Shailene the next.

When the crust of day started to show, I was already dressed and making a bare breakfast of toast and jam with coffee, intent on rejoining the search if there was still a need for one, when I heard the horses coming down the road.

Jonathan ran into the kitchen, trying to pull his shoes on while he used his feet. "Someone's here."

I took a deep breath and exhaled. "I know," is all I could bring myself to say.

We ran outside to the front lawn as my daddy and brothers rode up. The dust the horses riled up was almost suffocating this early, when the soft aroma of the morning dew was still fresh.

"What is it, Daddy?"

It felt like everything was frozen in time. Nobody spoke. They looked practically too scared to move. All except Daddy. He was the only one to dismount.

I asked, "Where did you find her?" He closed the distance between us until he stood directly in front of me. "You did find her." I didn't know whether I was saying it as a question or an order.

His lip trembled.

I began to shake my head. "No. You wouldn't stop looking if you didn't find her, Daddy. Tell me you found her."

He grabbed me into his arms so I couldn't see the shame in his eyes.

"We found her satchel. By the pond. The deep one."

I tried to keep my tone neutral. "That don't mean nothing."

"James found one of her shoes along the bank."

I shook my head frantically. "No."

When he spoke next, I heard it. I heard his worst fear coming to life when he said, tight-jawed, "Looks to be she fell in."

"No!" I wailed into his shoulder. "No!"

He refused to let go, squeezing as my body convulsed with grief.

"She can swim," I promised over and over again.

"Not like you and your brothers." He held me by my shoulders and looked me in the eyes. "You do understand, don't you? You know what I'm telling you, don't you, Nora?"

I tore from his grip. Through gritted teeth, I raised my head and stared right through him. "You're telling me lies. You're a liar."

Before he could finish saying, "I ain't," I sprinted through the yard, hopping the fence, and ran to my mare, Brownie.

A fire ripped through my mind, burning every part of who I was. Possessed by rage, I screamed, "Liars!"

Before anyone could stop me, Brownie jumped the fence, and we sped down the road faster than I'd ever ridden. Things passed by like flashes of lightning. The wind ripped at my eyes. And when I heard voices screaming behind me, it only made us take off so fast I thought we'd start flying any second.

When I reached the pond my daddy had been talking about, I didn't even stop Brownie before I dove off her back right into the murky water, breaking the film of green growth over top it.

I'd prove my sister wasn't in there. I planned to cover every inch of the deep pond before I'd stop. And if I found nothing, I planned to hop into the next one and prove them wrong again.

It didn't take long before they caught up to me. Jonathan

was riding with Dewey. The men dismounted in a fury and ran into the water after me. The horses snorted and whinnied, trotting out of the way.

"Nora!" Dewey pleaded. "Come on, now. This ain't no joke."

Jonathan couldn't swim, so he was left wading up to his knees, scared there would be a drop any next step. That's the thing about ponds in farming country. You never know just how deep they get. Some slope gently, never reaching impressive depths, while some drop a few feet at a time, creating notable pits. And you never truly know which is which until you get in.

The men waded deeper, struggling to catch up. Their bodies worked hard. But fall was a week away, and with it, the waters had already taken on a hard chill that wouldn't subside until next spring.

"Don't do this!" Jonathan shifted back and forth from one foot to the other, wishing beyond hope he could help. "Please, Nora, get out!"

James and his long legs started to draw closer. The nearer he got, the harder my arms strained to create more distance between us.

"Are you that dense?" James was yelling. "Get back here!"

I dove under before he could catch my arm. The splashing of his fists disrupting the water sent an alarming shudder down my spine. And then it was gone. I was gone.

I gave myself over to something greater, and it ate my fear.

The water felt like silk across my skin, the way Shailene's hair felt when it was first washed. It soothed me as I continued downward, arms outreached for anything in the dark abyss.

Down here, there was no light, no air, no lies. There was

weightless eternity. When I stopped fighting the anger in my heart, it was replaced with peace. A soft whisper echoed through the water.

And I heard a man call my name.

I had never heard such a voice before. It was laced with promises. Didn't matter if I was indifferent or wayward. Cruel or decent. Happy or desperate. Meek or boastful. He welcomed all.

My arms began floating to my sides rather than reaching forward. No longer persisting onward, a slight tilt racked my body, pulling my torso upward as my arms and legs hung limp awkwardly. The water could have been jelly encasing my skin.

A spark cried out in my brain, telling me not to believe this peace. It screamed at me to open my eyes. It fought most courageously to kick my legs.

It was losing.

Stillness crept in and the voice told me to let go.

The balance around me shifted suddenly as James dove down, sweeping me into his arms. Together, we shot upward, cresting the water. Everything turned offensively loud. They shouted all around me as James frantically dragged my limp body to the bank.

He glanced down at me, and as my eyelids fluttered open and closed, I recalled his expression, horror-stricken.

To my own surprise, it was Shailene who proved my brother, James, right. And his words wove in and out of my brain.

Ninety pounds can sink any man.

I had almost done just that. Almost killed my own brother. But it was his choice. No one made him do it. Some- where deep inside that vault of emotions, he had love for me, even a tiny bit, to have come for me.

James coughed something awful when we reached the bank, and he was able to collapse beside me. Daddy and the others gathered around us, rubbing my hands between theirs, trying to get me to answer their questions.

I ignored them all.

"Did you hear him?" I mumbled to James, my jaw unable to work properly. The ghost of a smile passed my lips.

Voice gruff, James asked, "Who?"

"Did he call your name, too?"

"I don't know what you're talking about. You about got us both killed, damn it."

Daddy shoved the other boys out of the way and kneeled beside me. "What did you say?"

Feeling like a mushy flapjack, I met Daddy's eyes. "I almost went. He said to."

"Who?" A knowledge graced his pained form, something he didn't want to say out loud. Maybe he regretted asking.

"It didn't feel so bad. I wasn't scared. When he said my name, I wasn't scared."

"You're talking crazy, girl. Who?" Leaning closer, eyes locked with mine, nearly begging, he asked, "Who was it?"

I just shook my head. "It don't matter, Daddy."

"The hell it don't, girl. Your brother's right. You just about got us all killed, following your antics."

But he knew. I could tell in his eyes, the way his voice wavered. He was scared, like he'd heard that voice, too. He wanted to know more, but he was fearful that I just might be able to tell him, so he let it go.

No one moved, afraid of what I might do next, I suppose. Look at that. A bunch of grown men, terrified. Maybe women were the stronger sex.

I sat up and coughed water out of my lungs.

"Where's my horse? Where's Brownie?" I demanded.

James sat up next to me, hugging his ribs. "What do you need a horse for? You ain't going anywhere."

Snapping, "The hell I'm not!" I pushed off James's shoulder and stumbled to my feet.

Jonathan grabbed my elbow to steady me.

"Nora May!" Daddy chastised. As quickly as it came, the rush of anger left him deflated. "I don't know what to do with you."

Jonathan and I headed toward Brownie. When I looked back at the sorry mess I'd created, I just shrugged. "You don't have to do nothing, Daddy. Except find my sister."

That was the last thing I said to my daddy for the next three months.

Jonathan helped me home that day. He watched over me when Rathe was out of town, becoming a second hand, a will that made me tend and get things done when I didn't have a will of my own to do it.

Talk started up in town. I was never sure whether Momma was heading the flock or whuping the scandalmongers. Any given day, I figured she could be one, the other, or both. Didn't bother us. Rathe liked knowing I was being looked after when he was away. And Jonathan liked having someone look after him. It made him miss his momma something terrible, though it also renewed his faith in that warm feeling you get when you know you're home just by being around a particular person.

He could also drive me to pull out every hair on my head some days.

"You gonna talk to your folks soon?" Jonathan asked.

"Wasn't planning on it."

"You should, you know."

"Not today."

"Yes, today."

"Not today," I'd keep saying.

A good daughter, a daughter like Shailene, would have pleaded for forgiveness from her folks for having the boldness to turn her back on them, even during her sister's own funeral. But I wasn't a good daughter. I was just me.

When Momma rode out and told me of Shailene's funeral arrangements after she went missing, I couldn't bear it. I hugged Momma, then sent her on her way with a promise. I wouldn't visit that damn stone until I discovered what horrible evil befell my sister, even if it meant never setting eyes on her grave. Momma was so shocked I expected her heart to give way right then and there.

That empty grave was an abomination to my sister's memory.

And it seemed for a time that they gave up on me. Jonathan never ceased to poke the boundaries of my repugnance for the entire topic, though.

"James almost drowned for you, Nora," Jonathan reminded me one fall day. "He's family. Don't turn your back on family. There's something unnatural about it."

Watching me make applesauce in the kitchen, Jonathan's favorite, he sat at the small table, hoping that part of me would wake up. The part that didn't care anymore.

They never did find Shailene. Daddy searched like no man before him. So did my brothers. Even Momma was seen from time to time wandering the paths, checking where she didn't believe eyes or legs had traveled.

Cutting the apples into small pieces, I shook my head. "I don't want to talk about it."

"You need to talk to somebody. I don't see it being your

momma. Especially not your daddy. You want me to round up James?"

"Hush up!" I threatened him, though the seriousness never manifested in my tone. More somber, I added, "James don't want any part of me. He made that clear."

"Right, like when he saved your life."

"I'm serious." I turned, pointing the tip of the knife blade in his direction. "Stop saying that." Waving the blade back and forth, I asked, "Now, do you want cinnamon in your apples or not."

"I never pass up cinnamon."

We shared a smile.

It was definitely nicer having Jonathan around when Rathe was off working. It filled the house with purpose. He had become like family to us. The entire Baker clan had. Rathe would hunt deer with Daryl and Colin. Jonathan was better at helping me and being handy on the homesteads rather than farming. He killed just about every plant he looked at, let alone touched, so we all thought it best if he stayed real far from the crops. And we couldn't wait for Colin and Dorthea to complete their courtship. She'd make a fine addition to their farm. Sweet and smart as all get-out.

"Are you going for a walk when you're done making that?" Jonathan wondered.

Nodding, I wiped the knife clean and set it beside the sink.

I still walked the fields on my own nearly every day, but it didn't hold the same wonder as before. Now, it was as if a sense of malevolence had sullied the qualities it once held. Somewhere along the way, it turned, ripened too much.

Even after my heart told me to stop, to let go, however, I kept walking.

I knew when James pulled me out of the pond that day. I

felt it sudden and thick, like poison constricting my chest, coursing through my heart. There was nobody that could tell me why or how. It just was. My sister was lost from this world.

And I was lost in it.

CHAPTER NINE

Plentiful

1925

Four years passed quicker than an eyelash disappearing in a furious wind, and Rathe was still waiting to be more than a family of two. No one needed to explain it to me. It had been eight years. By now, I didn't expect babies. Maybe it wasn't meant for us.

Momma had invited Preacher Smith out plenty of times to take stock of my soul, to make sure I wasn't at fault for our poor fortune. Of course, he didn't ever find nothing of interest. It would take a person of interest to have any type of ill-begotten fortune. That surely wasn't me.

Everyone was looking for reasons or blame for my barren state. Even Cousin Eula, who never had a kind word for anyone and would scarce pass up a chance to be spiteful, was using words like "poor" and "dear" anytime my name was referenced.

Truth be told, I was all right. Sadness didn't tug at my heart when I least expected it to. Nothing felt compromised or less fulfilling.

Fact was, I adored Rathe, and I was grateful for life on our little farm. My place had been marked in this world.

Right here, at home. The vegetables on our table were from my hands working the soil in our garden. The house was clean and snug because I spent more time than was necessary pouring love into it. We had all that we needed and then some. I was becoming the woman I had wished to be. Though, I found I wanted this more for myself than for Rathe's benefit.

It had taken an unholy amount of time to accept Shailene's loss. Rathe eventually quit his job in Henderson and took up carpentry, which allowed him the obvious comfort of being home more. Actually, it was more a necessity during the time after Shailene.

Once my brain and heart started working together again, I even took up visiting my folks. James and Able had married. And just like Daddy feared, Able had become a city man, living in Raleigh, of course. Suited him just fine. James picked a girl whose hard demeanor mirrored his own. They were something else entirely. Rathe didn't like being around them much. Said it gave him the heebie-jeebies to be around two people who were so alike it was downright unnerving.

Although everything had been flipped upside down and backward, it gave us all an opportunity to try harder. I never stopped loving Momma and Daddy, but I tried harder to show them. I did it wrong most of the time, I suspected. Just had to keep trying, let them know my heart was in it.

The season was unusually cool for August. Men in town were expecting an early winter, so Rathe and I stepped up our efforts to get everything ready. He was cutting extra wood, and I was tending to the house and garden. I was almost in a fitful possession when Jonathan mentioned how he'd seen the woman from his momma's funeral alongside the road earlier that day, trying to trade sewing work for food or extra material.

"Where is she now?" I asked, curiously, sweeping the kitchen.

"Home, I'd guess."

"Do you know where she lives?"

"Sure. North, half a mile past the two giant oaks on the left-hand side of the road."

"I'll be back. Here." I shoved the broom at him, and he barely caught it. Snatching up three full cans from my well-stocked canning shelves, I threw them in my satchel and took off, not really knowing what I had in mind to do.

Before I made it to the back door, I heard Jonathan mutter sarcastically, "Sure, I'll just stay here and clean. Borrow a dress while I'm at it."

I couldn't help but tease, "Take your pick. You'll look more like a lady in them than I ever will." Giggling, I left.

Taking the better half of an hour, I came across the two oaks and found a tiny cabin not far after.

"Hello!" I called from my horse.

No answer.

Stepping down and grabbing the cans, I adjusted my blouse and riding pants. Momma hated my riding pants. Threatened to burn them on more than one occasion. I don't know why, other than vanity. They were the best thing for living on a farm or riding.

Walking to the door, I patted my hair flat with my right hand and knocked on the thick surface.

A bit of rustling was heard on the other side.

"Hello? It's Nora Cravis. We met a few years ago."

The loud clink of a bar being removed made me take a step back.

The door inched open and a woman, the same woman I

remembered, though much thinner, peered out, her eyes squinted.

"Hi," I greeted.

She nodded once. "Hello."

"We were both at Widow Baker's funeral." When she didn't respond, I added, "I brought you some extra canned goods for winter."

Not reaching for them as I held them extended between us, her eyes shifted from them to me.

"What would give you such an impression that we need your handout?"

Her attitude was borderline indignant, her words stretched out as she tried to enunciate each one with her heavy Spanish accent.

I shrugged. "My friend passed you on the road earlier. Said you were asking for work."

"So you bring canned tomatoes and green beans?"

"I don't have money to pay you for any work. Do you want them or not? I rode a long way to bring them here."

"And I did not ask you to do such a thing."

I about pulled my arm away, but I heard a tiny voice from inside ask, "Mama, can we eat now?"

She drew in a breath and took the cans out of my hands. Staring at the ground, she smiled and said, "Thank you. Would you like to come in?"

The door opened wider, and I stepped into the dim room.

"Your name's Luz, isn't it?"

"Yes. This is Raymond."

I found little Raymond, not yet five if I were correct, trying to force one of the cans open.

"It's stuck," he told me, holding it up for help.

I popped the green beans open and gave them to Luz,

who poured a small pile into the middle of a plate and set it down in front of the child. He ate it right then and there, cold, with no fuss.

"So he's Raymond Colt's son." There wasn't no question.

Luz nodded.

"Why'd you name him after a man who didn't treat you so kindly?"

Thinking quietly for a minute, she answered, "Because everyone deserves to have love, even if it is just in a name."

I sat down and thought about what she'd said. And I wondered whether Jonathan or his brothers would have half as much forgiveness as this woman.

Her full, dark skirt brushed over the floor almost as if she were floating on the air itself. Her blouse was rich with so many colors. It almost detracted from the dark circles around her eyes. She looked quite ragged from the first time I saw her in church. Her skin had glowed, her hair thick and shiny. I understood this new look, though. It was desperation. It was too many chores and not enough hours. It was too many hours and not enough hands.

"How are you doing out here? You two alone?"

Luz nodded.

"Farmers in town are saying it's gonna be a bad winter. My husband and I are about caught up with our farm. If you'll be needing any help, we can give it."

"Why would you help me?" She was truly interested.

Pulling the door open, I shrugged. "Because we can, I guess." As I mounted Brownie, I called out, "I'll send my husband over in the next few days to brace your barn for the winter weather. It won't hold the way it is now."

She just nodded from the door and waved. I think she was hopeful that I'd stick to my word.

I waved and rode home.

That evening, I discussed my plan with Rathe.

"You want me to ride all the way out there to help some woman we don't even know? Whose man killed your best friend's momma?"

Picking at my food on the plate, I set my fork down. "Well, when you say it like that, it don't sound like such a great idea."

"So you agree with me." He shoved a chunk of meat in his mouth.

"No. You get your tail out there tomorrow."

Swallowing his food, Rathe shook his head. "Why we got to save everyone? We practically adopted Jonathan." He turned his head toward the counter. "No offense."

"None taken," Jonathan assured him as he kept shoveling food into his mouth.

"Jonathan, does it bother you that I want to help your momma's killer's son and his momma? You know you can speak honest with me." I waited, holding my breath for the right answer. Or rather, for the answer I wanted to be right.

Jonathan shook his head. "It don't bother me none."

Rathe turned around again. "Why not?"

He shrugged. A habit he picked up from me. "I guess because I don't blame them. Raymond Colt was a son of a bitch who stole my momma's life right out from under us. But no one can carry that blame but him."

I smiled. Hearing Jonathan talk like that was reassuring that good people were alive and well in this world. Everything he loved was stolen from him in the span of a bullet. He just kept loving rather than let that bullet kill him a little every day.

Rathe pushed his plate away and sat back in the chair, thinking.

When his eyes fell on me, I said, "That woman needs help. She's sinking fast."

He nodded. "Then we'll help."

That's how my sisterhood with Luz Ravera started.

And when I almost lost my husband.

CHAPTER TEN

In The Light Of Day
1925-1926

"*L*uz needs you again when you've got time," I mentioned as we pulled the covers aside and slid into bed.

Rathe stretched out, rubbing his hands through his hair and down his face. "I've been out there a lot lately."

"Is it bothering you to go?" I rolled over, facing him, my head lying on the crook of my arm.

"I guess not. People are starting to talk, though. I don't like it."

"People always talk. If they stopped, they might forget how to be people."

He closed his eyes. "I think I'd like that for a while."

"I've been thinking..." I was worried how Rathe would react to my idea, so I just blurted it out in the open. "That cabin ain't gonna last much longer without a serious hand."

He grunted in agreement.

"What if Luz sold it, got the money while there's something workable to sell, and...moved here with us?"

"What?" Rathe sat straight up, shaking his head, waving his hands. "Holy God, Nora, people gonna think I done married twice. I can't have two grown women under one roof. She ain't family!"

"Well, neither is Jonathan, but we made him family." I sat up and grabbed his hand in mine. "Luz is no different. She and Raymond could be happy here."

"It ain't her house," he whined, pulling his hand free.

"Could be." Lying down, I rolled over, turning my back to Rathe, and added, "There was a time it weren't my house, either."

"Oh!" he moaned, falling backward until his body bounced into the bed. "I'm sure Luz can be happy right where they are. Why is this so important to you?"

"Because..." My voice choked in my throat.

When Rathe realized I was fighting back tears, he propped up on his elbow and leaned over me, whispering, "Tell me what's wrong." He rubbed his cheek in my hair slowly.

"When I'm with Luz, that part of me that I thought was gone or blackened out forever kind of sparks, like maybe there's hope that a piece of my heart didn't really die off and shrivel away."

I had cried every day for a year after losing Shailene, but this was the first tear Rathe had seen fall in her memory. It was my best-kept secret. I cried while milking the cows, and scrubbing the floors, and beating the rugs. But never when anyone was truly watching.

Rathe nodded. "Worst thing in my life is watching you grieve. You don't do it the way everyone else grieves. They're angry and they cry and spit at the world. But you... It rips a piece of you away from me every day. And it has, Nora, every day for the last four years."

I hadn't realized he was watching so close, studying me and getting to know me so well. Wanting to say something, like apologize, or tell him I could be better, I rolled onto my back, looking up at him, and started to interrupt his sweet words.

Instead, he held up his hand. "Don't. You don't need to make excuses to me. I ain't your folks." He leaned down and kissed me on the lips.

When he leaned back, I said, "I don't want you to think I ain't happy here. I am. If I didn't have you or this farm, I wouldn't have survived." I clasped his hands to my chest. "My heart would have crumbled to dust and blown to the four corners without you."

Rolling onto his back, Rathe crossed his arms behind his head.

"I guess we better make room. They aren't the two additions I was hoping to make to our family, but I can't say no. Not now." Before I could say anything, he added, "But you might feel different about it in the light of day. Sleep on it tonight. If you feel the same way in the morning, well then, that's what we're doing."

My soul felt like singing. I was so happy I hardly slept all night, counting the minutes until I could ask my friend this very important question.

Unable to stand it a moment longer, I was up and dressed long before the sun rose, putting me right at Luz's door as the sky lightened and gave to the dawn.

"Is there something wrong?" She waved me inside.

"Oh, Luz, only if you say no."

"I can make coffee," Luz offered.

I swatted her off with my hands.

"Listen, sit down." When we sat at their bare table, I took a breath and said, "Rathe and I have been talking. About the future. What do you think about selling your cabin and coming to stay with us?"

"Sell our cabin?" Luz was confused at first, unable to make sense of my offer.

"You'd keep any gains from selling the place. We aren't asking for your money. It's just, it's a lot for one person." I peered over at Raymond, tucked away soundly in bed, his little cherub mouth hanging open as he slept. "One and a quarter," I amended, smiling.

"Nora, you are thoughtful and kind, but we cannot. What would others say?"

"Why is everyone so worried about what other people are saying? They've been talking my whole life. Hasn't bit me in the tail yet. Hasn't ruined nothing for me."

Luz pulled her loose shawl tighter around herself and sat in quiet.

I guess I understood. It wasn't something people did by choice unless they were family, or falling on hard times. Luz and Raymond wanted for a lot, but they had a roof and enough food. Luz had recently taken on some sewing projects that promised a secure winter for them. What then? Was just getting by real living, or was it just fighting for that last breath every single day?

Standing, I readied to leave, politely saying, "I wasn't trying to put you in an awkward position, and I don't blame you for staying."

Before I made it to the door, Luz rushed over.

"Why would you invite us into your home?"

I shrugged. "Because you're already in my heart."

Luz mustered the largest smile I'd ever witnessed from her usually serious demeanor. "Yes, we will accept your kind gesture."

Not a month later, Luz and Raymond sold that albatross of a homestead and came to stay with us. They tucked quite nicely into the second bedroom. Raymond was still small enough to share a bed with Luz, but Rathe had it in his mind to build him a little bed all to his own. There was an expression on Rathe's face when he announced his idea. It was jubilation. In that moment, I never realized just how deeply his heart had yearned to craft anything for small fingers and small toes.

It sure was different having a little thing ramming his way through us to get to what he wanted, and grabbing every chance he got to voice his mind. Luz often apologized, thinking he was unruly. For us, it was something different entirely. He was a pleasant curiosity. It was hard to mind his momma and tell him no when all we wanted to do was make him happy. And he was sure excited when Rathe started letting him help care for the animals. They worked side by side for hours at a time.

"This does not bother you?" Luz asked one day as she cleaned the dishes. Peering out the tiny window, she watched Raymond take large steps behind Rathe, trying his best to keep up with him.

Laughing, I kept mashing the potatoes for dinner. "That's silly. No, it makes me awfully happy."

Setting a large pot in the sink, she turned around and crossed her arms. "You are very different from anyone I have met."

"I'm hoping that's meant as a compliment. Wouldn't be like you to insult a woman in her own home." I couldn't help myself. A sly grin crept over my lips as I added, "That's my momma's job."

"She has many jobs. Supervisor. Boss. Chief."

We both giggled.

Her serious tone returned rather quickly, though. "You should talk to your mother."

"I talk to Momma plenty. It would do my mental faculties more good if I talked to her less. I don't see her allowing that to happen."

"No, speak to her from your heart, not with jokes."

Finding myself smashing the potatoes with the strength of Hercules, I set the bowl down and stretched my fingers. "Why is this so important to you?"

"You are a good friend to me. You have helped us. Let me be a good friend to you. I can help, too."

"I appreciate your concern, Luz, but there's nothing to help with when it comes to my momma and daddy. Shailene was our bridge to understand each other. After... Well, we can't make ourselves be different just for each other. That ain't fair to any of us."

Her agitation was clear when she began to scold me. "You are old." Pointing to my chest, she said, "You are old in there. Set in your ways, like them." Shaking her head with disapproval, she noted, "All you have to do is try. Do not try to be a different person. Try to embrace the love you share. With love will come what you need from one another."

It wasn't that she was saying anything different from what I'd already promised myself in the past to do more of. Of course I should show Momma and Daddy love. They didn't often make it an easy task. Then again, I was never one for taking the easy road.

Luz was only saying what I had been thinking for a long time. She just made it sound easier, and I let my frustration win over for a bit.

She turned around and began to clean the dishes again. We worked in silence up until dinner. Rathe and Jonathan ate like horses, all the while making faces, causing food to fall out of Raymond's mouth every time they made him squeal or yell, "More!" Luz and I tried our best not to find it amusing.

It wasn't until Luz passed the potatoes that I looked her in the eyes and smiled. "You were right."

"I know."

"You're not much on modesty," Jonathan noted with amusement.

Luz smiled. "Not when I am right."

After a moment's hesitation, we all laughed. Even little Raymond, although he wasn't sure what we found so hilarious. He just didn't want to be left out.

We had many dinners like that, the five of us. Sometimes Jonathan's brother, Daryl, joined us. Those evenings were extra special because it helped Luz set to rest the hard past they shared. And although Colin had been the first to forgive her at their momma's funeral, he couldn't bring himself to share a table with her. Not yet.

I knew that would change one day, though, because Luz and her little one were already so much a part of our lives.

There was a familiarity and comfort from having Luz and Raymond in our home. They ingrained into daily life with ease, enriching every experience. Luz shared her cultural heritage, making sure that little Raymond could speak her country's language, and we began teaching him how to read and write in English. He would be the most well-versed boy in two languages by the time we were done with him. That's what we hoped for, at any rate.

An entire year passed faster than a sprout growing into a mighty stalk. As Raymond grew, so did our hearts. He had become the heartbeat of our home. And it was *our* home. All of ours. The human heart can't survive much grief without fracturing, but it sure has the power to stretch unending with love. I think we had all begun to heal in our own special ways. There was no doubt.

Funny how you find what you want in something you

didn't expect to have.

"Summer's about over. I can feel a change in the air."

The air was tinged with the faint smell of dense brush. It stuck in the back of your throat at times, barely noticeable other times. It only subsided once the leaves started their seasonal journey.

"It was a good summer," Luz affirmed. After a few minutes passed, she carefully said, "Can I ask you a question?"

"You can ask me anything."

Luz surprised me when, making no apologies, she asked, "Does having Raymond here make you wish for a child of your own?"

Sitting with Luz in the weathered lean-to captured the memories of me and Shailene sitting there so many times before, wearing our thoughts inside out.

I swallowed, thinking on it. "No."

Luz was curious. She was often confused by my feelings. Maybe because she felt everything so passionately and with conviction, while I gathered the world up and sifted it back out bit by bit.

"A lot of women I know describe motherhood as a tug or yearning they can't escape. It grows in them long before they carry their babies." I shrugged. "It just doesn't exist in me." When she didn't respond, I asked, "Did you feel it?"

An air of woe fell over Luz. A mood I had yet to witness from her.

Sitting calmly, I waited, because I had learned to be patient. Luz often took her time to think about her words before she spoke them out loud. Partly because she prided herself on speaking exceptionally good English, and partly because she wasn't about to waste her words on thoughts she didn't believe in.

"Yes." Nodding, she went on. "It was not a tug, as you say. More of a truth that would come to pass. A want so deep I did not see it as a want, only a when."

She continued milking as she talked. "Before Raymond, I had a baby daughter." Looking my way through the corner of her eyes, she said, "I have never spoken of her with you."

I shook my head, confirming.

"I was a young girl in Monterrey, merely pretending to be a woman. Juan was no older. Every day, I stared at the Cerro de la Silla, dreaming of having my own home with the same view of my precious mountain. Juan agreed there was to be a future between us." Her brow wrinkled as she was haunted by memories. "Married and round with child, Juan grew restless with a new purpose. He refused to ignore the need, so overwhelming, to join the Revolución Mexicana and died while fighting by Pancho Villa's side."

"He left you to fight in a war?"

"To help release our people from the rule of Porfirio Díaz. I have yet to meet any man who loves more fully than Juan. His country or his family. He was trying to make a finer life for our daughter. She was born small, and disease was unavoidable. Our life together was short, but full. With both of my loves."

The way she recited her past with a sense of detachment said more than her words. If you're busy telling a story, focusing on the words, you ain't got time to feel the pain as deep as it wants to run.

"I'm sorry for you," I whispered.

The struggling emotions within her continued for some time. Slowly, we both continued to milk until Luz found her voice again.

"I apologize."

I was surprised. "For what, living? For not having control

over the world?"

A fringe of a smile caught her expression. "It was a much different life in Mexico. Some moments better. Some not."

She sighed.

"I can't imagine. I've only ever been here, and over there a little, and over that way a little."

We laughed a bit.

"There is a worldly way that your soul speaks to people. That is a greater treasure than being in many places."

"Thank you," I said, taken aback by such a compliment.

"You do well with Raymond. I wish mi hermosita were here for you to meet."

Raymond was a joy I never counted on. It hurt my heart to think there could have been two sets of laughter filling the space between these walls.

"Me, too, Luz. I wish with more might than the sun's strength that your daughter could be with us right now."

She smiled wide. "I know. That's what sets you apart, your ability to love somebody, to know a part of them, without ever meeting them. I will say a prayer for you, asking for many children, if that is what you secretly wish for."

I shook my head. "No, Luz. It's been so long now, there's no baby feet in my future. I'm well and truly good with that. It ain't meant for me and Rathe. It doesn't stop us from pouring every bit of love into Raymond, though."

We carried the milk pails down to the back door. Before walking inside, I hugged Luz tightly. She was never one to break open her torments like a wayward seedpod spilling its valuables into the green universe. It was hard on her. Maybe because she had survived hard times.

Well, times were about to get harder. We were having dinner with my family.

CHAPTER ELEVEN

A Mighty Fall
1926

*R*athe, Luz, Raymond, and I pulled up outside Momma and Daddy's in the wagon the same time Cousin Eula and her beau arrived in the most dramatic fashion. The horses shuffled about as we heard a horn reminiscent of a sickly duck grow ever closer behind us. Every one of us about jumped out of our skin.

Raymond hopped up and yelled, "Mama, look!"

They pulled up in a black vehicle with no top. Cousin Eula was grasping her cloche hat from all angles to keep it steady, all the while forcing a smile as they raced up beside us before coming to a jarring halt.

A man dressed like fortune had hit twice waved as he ran around to open Cousin Eula's door and help her out.

"Why thank you," she gushed.

We all hopped out of the wagon and said our hellos. Cousin Eula's gentleman was named Barney. He was definitely city.

Rathe eyed the contraption with a mixture of curiosity and amusement. "What do you got there?"

The man slapped the front of the vehicle. "This here's a Model T Roadster." When Rathe failed to swoon or jump about in a frenzy, the stranger noted, "Ford. Best of the best."

Cousin Eula rested her arm through his and shook her head. Like a secret we could all hear, she said, "They don't appreciate modern conveniences the way we do."

I stared at her and answered flatly, "I've seen vehicles before."

"Oh, I know, Nora." Walking past, she whispered sweetly, "Just not up close."

She had been seeing Barney for the better half of a year. I wasn't sure what he saw in her, but I was positive he wasn't in any way mentally incapacitated, so his feelings toward her must be true if he'd made it this far.

Having relocated to Durham about the time Luz and Raymond came to stay with us, Cousin Eula had only made it home to visit Aunt Virgie once a season. This time, however, I was betting she had special news 'cause it was the first time Barney had accompanied her.

Walking inside, Momma and Daddy greeted everyone, and Momma popped Daddy in the gut right good when he wanted to know where the rest of Cousin Eula's dress had gone.

She was in a red, knee-high, sleeveless dress with a scoop neck that would have made a man of God change alignment. Upon Daddy's rudeness, she only laughed, taking it as a compliment that she didn't look like the rest of us no more. She was definitely city now. And she definitely wanted it that way.

When Daddy met Barney, he asked, "What do you do? You're dressed too nice to be a farmer, and she's dressed too nice to be a farmer's wife."

"Insurance," he responded cheerfully.

Looking out the window at the machine sitting in front like an eyesore, Daddy sat back in his chair in the living room and grunted, as if to say, "Figures."

Luz and I left Raymond to jump between the men on the couch while we went in back to help Momma in the kitchen. Cousin Eula was already there, draped across a section of the counter. The fabric pulled across her midsection, leaving nothing to the imagination.

The rest of us were in our usual attire, having seen better days. The aprons hid most of the blemishes in the fabric that made up my loose cotton dress. Not that I had made an effort to do different from always.

When Luz reached past Cousin Eula to grab a dish from the cabinet, I saw my cousin eye her with a bit of disdain. I think she was feeling replaced. I don't know why. Luz was capable of preparing, cooking, and cleaning up after a meal. Cousin Eula had yet to prove she possessed the necessary skills to do the same.

"So," Momma ho-hummed, "you've never brought a suitor to visit. I'm assuming there's a reason."

When she and Cousin Eula's gazes met, they both smiled like they used up every bit of strength and joy all at once.

"Nothing official," she confided. "But he's been talking a lot more about his future plans, and I'm mentioned quite a bit."

"How exciting. I knew things would change when you moved to Durham." Momma smiled again as she returned to scrubbing the vegetables.

I asked, "Are you still making pantyhose?"

Cousin Eula gasped. "You make it sound like I'm

grueling away in some dull factory next to a million girls who all blend into the same background."

"I think you are the one who made it sound like that," Luz commented.

She had not spent much time around Cousin Eula, but the moments they had shared were burned into her memory as distinctly abysmal.

"I didn't," she protested.

"If you say so."

I fought the tiny smile that wanted to blossom.

"Anyway, I'm not working the line anymore. I've been promoted."

Momma stopped to say with heart, "Well, that's excellent."

"I'm helping in the office now. Surely, if so many colored folks can own businesses now, it might be possible that women can be trusted to help run somebody else's."

I peered at Luz from the corners of my eyes as she did the same to me. The difference between Cousin Eula and every business owner, colored or otherwise, was, she didn't have no dern sense, while they built everything they had from dust to gold with honest work and know-how.

Sighing, I said, "It takes everything you got to make something, cousin."

She nodded, as if I'd read a passage from the Bible she dun wrote herself. "Barney and I will have more than enough in the bank to do whatever we like in the future."

Luz shook her head. "Anyone can use money. Buy, buy, buy. Do you have what it takes in here," she motioned to her chest, "to give value to what you do?"

"What is wrong with you?" she snorted at Luz.

"Nothing," I spat back, flicking a piece of batter at her face.

"Why can't I have one decent meal with you, Nora May?" She looked as though she might cry. The batter fell from her forehead with a light thud to the ground.

"We ain't starting this again!" Momma warned. "You're grown, the lot of you."

Daddy walked through the doorway, rubbing his hands together, ready to ask when dinner would be on the table. The spark fled, however, when he saw the scowls on our faces and the food on the floor.

"Aw, hell." He turned around and we could hear him, in a downcast tone, telling the men, "It's gonna be a while."

"Look, you gone and depressed your daddy."

"I can't be held responsible for Daddy's stomach, too," I stated.

My momma looked at me more serious than ever. "Nora, what do you need?"

"What do you mean?" I set the mixing bowl down and just stood there.

"What do you need to heal yourself?" Momma asked sincerely. "If I can give it, by God, I'll hand it over right now. If I could buy it, steal it, make it, I'd do it right this minute if it was in my control."

All eyes fell to me.

Momma's brow furrowed, and I could suddenly see how she'd aged the last few years.

"You can't keep on taking it out on us, baby. You just can't. We got our own healing to do."

It irked me something terrible to acknowledge that Momma was speaking the truth. It wasn't right to treat my family so poorly at times. I was still devastated over the loss of Shailene. Blinded in many ways.

I didn't miss her because she was my sister and best friend. I missed the empty space of her secrets. The silly questions she always managed to ask out loud. Knowing more of what each other meant in our silence than what we were trying to say with our words. The feeling of knowing and being known so well it just felt like a part of living.

The real lie was living without her.

When a loss permeates your flesh and bone and burrows right into your soul, and you can't make no sense of why you lost them... It breeds hate. This hatred becomes a fire you walk on, no matter where you go. Nothing can extinguish it.

Where'd all the hate come from? I don't think it was there before. It took over the space in my heart when the grief became too great. When my loneliness without Shailene turned into a numb limb that couldn't be cut off.

After the longest quiet Momma's kitchen had ever witnessed, I turned to Cousin Eula.

Could I fix this mess? Could it be reconciled with them, with myself?

"Eula..." I started to say, "it pains me that you think I'm jealous of you. Since we were little, you never really saw me, and I never cared to try harder."

She didn't quite know how to respond. "I wouldn't say that," she concluded.

"No, I'm saying it. I'm different. I know it, but it doesn't bother me like it does you or Momma or Daddy, or anybody else."

Momma, in a soft tone, asked, "What do you want from Eula?"

"I want you to be happy because you've got your life and not mine. And I'll be happy because I've got my life and not yours. So let's be happy for each other. No more pity."

When she straightened her posture, the red dress

swooshed about her like it had its own mind. There seemed to be a subtle awakening in Cousin Eula. It gave me hope. "Okay," she finally said, nodding. "As long as you stop throwing things at me."

In all honesty, I promised, "I will try my best." Smiling, I motioned toward the living room. "Barney's been in there with Daddy an awful long time. If he didn't try to run away, you might want to marry him."

She smiled wide. "I've got so many reasons to marry that man, I don't need one more."

We managed to cook the rest of the meal and eat it without incident. And, to our shock, we took a shine to Barney. He may have been a big city talker, but he came from farming roots close to Stem, and held a great deal of respect for people like Daddy, working to the bone for an honest day's wage. We sat in the living room and listened to Momma and Daddy's radio the boys had chipped in together to buy them. Barney knew a lot about it. He'd even met a few of the radio personalities, as they called them. There was even programming purely for women.

After that, Barney took Raymond for a long ride in the Ford. The little one had never ridden in a vehicle before, and talked about nothing else the rest of the evening.

As we gathered on the front porch to say our goodbyes, hugging and wishing everybody well, I came to Momma last.

It took every bit of guts I could muster to hug her and say, "It's my turn to tell you what I need from you, Momma."

"Anything."

A hush fell about as I requested simply, "I need for you to tell me the truth. I need to know about Shailene."

She understood that I was asking not only on behalf of

Shailene's disappearance, but the events that preceded. This matter followed me like a shadow from sunup to sunset and inspired my harshest nightmares.

Blinking her eyes more than necessary, wasting time, a kind of strength came over her. I had never quite seen it before. This must have been Momma's inner hardness coming to the surface. We all had it, but God willing, most of us never had to use it. Not against our own kin.

"Can you tell me, Momma? Not now, I mean, but if I come back alone, will you tell me what you know? Please." My last word was little more than a strangled breath.

The muscles in her jaw clenched and unclenched as she curtly shook her head once.

"I can't do that," she informed me. Saying nothing more to any of us, she turned around and withdrew inside. Don't get me wrong, she wasn't running. She was just done. With every dark word concerning Shailene that no one seemed able to speak out loud.

Daddy walked over and hugged me stiffly. When he let go, he cleared his throat. "Some things ain't meant to be said aloud. Set your momma free from this. Don't ask for something she can't give you."

My daddy's nerve about enraged me. I struggled to keep my eyes from bugging out of my head and my mouth shut, not wanting to say anything that couldn't be taken back.

Catching a glimpse of my thoughts, he leaned in. "It can't be," he urged me.

His words stuck with me for the rest of that evening, all the way up to the following afternoon as I was sitting on the front steps, shucking corn, while Raymond napped and Luz was around back.

It can't be.

"Only 'cause you refuse," I mumbled under my breath.

Luz was walking around the corner, holding a large basket to cradle the sticks and small branches as she picked them up from the ground. They made perfect kindling for the fire.

"Why can you not let it rest?" she asked gently.

"Because she was stolen out of my life, and I can't make any sense of it on my own. I've tried up and down and backward. It's taken up residence in every inch of my skin. It runs through my brain whether I want to think on it or not. And my heart! My heart just shudders 'cause it's incapable of handling any of it." I dropped everything and stared at her. "Not without answers."

"Maybe the answers you seek do not exist."

"Daddy and Momma see what it's done to me and still won't help. They have answers, all right. If someone was stolen from you, you wouldn't be asking me to let it rest."

Luz's posture shifted. She slammed the basket of sticks to the ground and balled her hands into fists at her sides.

"You should feel ashamed to act like your heart is the only one to know this pain. My daughter's life was stolen from me. My baby! When she grew sick, I had no way to help her. I needed money. I wasn't even there to see her last breath. I was buying bread for the sisters... But I hear her cries!" she wailed. "I hear them, still. Sometimes I wake to them, reaching for her. And with each outstretched arm, I must accept that she is gone. I must feel it over and over, because pain does not disappear as easily as the bodies we yearn to hold close."

I sat on the steps, crying silently.

"Your parents do with their knowledge the best way they can. Have faith in them. You can accuse them, you can be angry, but their pain will never disappear with their daughter. And it is unfair to act as if it already has simply because you have your own pain." She practically screamed, "We all have our own pain!"

Kneeling to pick up the basket and sticks, she uttered, "You cannot let pain and anger live your life or it will be worthless. I know this. I had many worthless years before Raymond."

I wanted to reply, to say anything, but I wasn't given the chance. Jonathan rode up in a feverish whirlwind, the hooves of his brown and white appaloosa kicking dirt and rocks every which way. He yelled, "Come on! Something happened!" before the horse ever came to a standstill.

"What's going on?" I stood up.

"A man came into town. Said there was an accident at the Miller ranch. He was fetching a doctor and as many hands that could follow him."

"Did they say who?"

Not wanting to, he nodded. "I wouldn't be here if I weren't sure."

Rathe had been working long days on a barn with two other men at the Miller ranch. When I'd last seen him, he kissed me as I handed him the lunch he almost forgot.

My chest pounded. My heart couldn't figure out whether it needed to beat more or whether it wasn't beating enough. The rhythm contributed to the sick feeling in my gut.

Running to Jonathan's appaloosa, I tripped over my loose shoes. Summersaulting to the ground, one flew off in the ruckus. I only took a moment to realize that every second spent wasting time on shoes was a second longer I was away from Rathe. And he needed me. By God, I didn't know why, but I wasn't about to waste time finding out.

Kicking the other one off, still wearing my riding pants and raggedy chore shirt, I turned back to Luz.

"Go!" she assured me. "We will take care here."

Mutely, I took Jonathan's outstretched hand and hopped on. He got the mare back on the road with no explanation.

The ride was too long. Too much time lapsing, causing my mind to fret harder with each passing tree, bridge, dog, cow... I wrapped my arms tighter around Jonathan's torso, using each hoofbeat as a wish.

Be okay.

Don't leave me.

Stay strong.

Wait for me.

The afternoon was about past when we rode up to the Miller property.

Men were running, taking orders from a voice whose body I couldn't yet see. Horses were still hitched to wagons, unattended. Nobody thought nothing of us riding in like Satan was upon us.

Jumping to my feet, I asked, "Where?"

Jonathan took my hand, and we ran past the men and their tools, past the main house and cow barn, until we came to an alienating structure. I couldn't quite make out what it was supposed to be because it didn't match nothing around it. Exposed beams hung with an ailing tilt. There was no roof where there clearly had once been one. And the smell of soaking, rotting wood and pungent mildew wafted from the entire mess.

Someone with a booming voice commanded, "Let's go, men! There's no time left. He ain't talking no more."

The air left my lungs in one swift motion. *Did they mean Rathe? He wasn't talking?* Time started catching, slowing to a crawl as I watched the pure chaos panic was causing. I wanted to run to Rathe, wherever he was, but time was holding me back.

Jonathan bounded up to the shaggy-headed man and pointed to me. I didn't wait to be called on. Breaking free of time's lingering grasp, I entered the scene with a new confidence.

"Where is he?" I demanded. "Take me to him now." I walked past them, expecting them to catch up and show me.

The man did just that.

"Are you his wife, ma'am?"

"Do I look like his momma?"

"My name's Henry." He grabbed his hat and nodded once.

I was confused. I thought we were in the middle of an emergency, not a church social. I leveled my voice, strong and solid, and reminded him, "You said it. We ain't got time. Show me, now!"

He could tell I wasn't lollygagging, and probably wasn't the best to irritate under the circumstances, which were yet to be uncloaked.

Walking swiftly, side by side, I followed his lead when he walked into the shady structure and stopped short of a catawampus pile of wood beams and debris.

"I don't understand. What is this? Where's Rathe?"

Another man who had been standing there as we walked up pointed to the pile. "He's in there, ma'am." His voice was shaky. "The whole dang thing collapsed. Rotten, every bit of it."

Searching the angles and textures creating the garbled mess in front of me, I finally saw him. It was Rathe, nothing but softness in the middle of an inflexible horror. At that moment, looking at him under a pile of rubble, I realized I had been holding out hope that they were mistaken. That they'd accidentally confused him with someone else. Anybody.

The anxious man kept saying, "I'm sorry. He hasn't moved in an awful long time. I'm sorry, ma'am."

"Stop it," I said under my breath.

Inhaling and exhaling loudly, he kept on. "It ain't good. He ain't moving. Hadn't said nothing the better part of an hour. It ain't good."

"Stop it!" I charged, this time much louder.

Jonathan stepped up beside me. "They're gathering rope to set up a pulley." Struck silent for a moment, he reformed his thoughts so he could finally tell me, "Those beams weigh more than we can lift on our own. You get what I'm saying? They're heavier than a pile of horses."

That was Jonathan's way of telling me those beams had most likely just crushed the life out of the man who'd sat in our kitchen, kissing my bare feet, promising never to leave me.

And I wasn't permitting talk like that.

The men began rallying around, hurling rope this way and that, trying to decide as quick as possible the best angles for the job. As they fluttered about, I stood as close to Rathe as the rotten beams would allow. The light shined down through the hole, right on top of us. Like maybe there were angels gathering around us, discussing Rathe's fate, making sense of the devastation. Maybe I was a fool, but I got real still and held my breath, hoping I could hear something. When I didn't, I shut my eyes tight and whispered, "Don't take him."

About that time, I heard Daddy and James's voices traveling through the barn. I didn't leave Rathe, though. Staring at his slack expression, his mouth hanging partly open, the tension at the sides of his eyes absent, I could see what he must have looked like as a boy. No worries or demons. Just...the light of his soul shining through.

James barked, "Hook up the first beam. Now, now, now!" He slammed his hands together, creating a piercing clap that was impossible for anyone to ignore.

"Step to it!" Daddy yelled behind him. "Man's life is in your hands!"

I felt as though I stood there longer than it took the world to come into being, waiting as they pulled one beam after another off Rathe's fragile form. There was no way of describing the utter terror surging through my thoughts. My brain froze up when it became too overwhelming.

I was waiting on reality to set in. But which reality: the old one, the only one I wanted, or a brand-new one that seemed unbearably lonesome?

When the men shifted the last of the beams, we were able to see that Rathe had fallen between two of the braces, protecting him from the brunt of the force.

Scurrying barefoot across the wood, I suffered minor scratches and splinters, of which I disregarded. As I reached Rathe, every man there fell as still and silent as a grave. Because, for every beam they had removed, Rathe remained motionless, unaware of their mighty efforts.

I crouched down beside him, rubbing his cheek with my palm.

"Rathe, if I ask one thing of you in this moment, you gotta do it, okay? Out of my selfishness and cruelness, you can't *not* listen, okay?" Brushing his wavy hair away from his forehead with my fingertips, I said, "I need you to wake up now." Fighting back the tears that had been invoked, I continued to plead, "You don't have to walk out of here on your own, and you don't have to feel okay. I just need you to live."

Everyone waited.

Swallowing the hard lump in my throat, I watched him, my hope plummeting every second he failed to answer.

"God damn it," I whispered, "I swear I'll tell Him to send you to Hell if you don't do this for me. Wake up right now, Rathe." I slapped him across his slack face. "You swore forever in that church, holding my hand." I slapped him again. "You swore forever in our kitchen that I'd always be coming home to you."

After a third slap, James stepped forward, only a bit. "Nora, you can't make a man hold to such promises. He ain't got it in him."

"Don't you dare!" I screamed, standing to gain balance. "You once accused me of having the power to bring ruin and wreckage merely by being me. Ninety pounds can sink any man. You remember that?"

Every bit of tension rested on his bowed brow as he nodded.

"May-be." Inhaling deeply, I resolved, "Maybe I can sink a man. Well, I'm gonna show you right now, I can damn well bring one back, too."

Crouching over Rathe again, I grabbed the front of his shirt and twisted it in my fist. Between gritted teeth, I said, "Rathe, get up. You open your eyes right now if you don't want me to call on God, Lucifer, and everything in between to pull this world by the tail and hit you with it."

There was a slight noise, and everyone froze, listening.

I heard it again and leaned closer, only a foot away from Rathe's face.

"You can do it. Open your eyes and look at me." My voice cracked, but I refused to cry.

There must have been a miracle called in by everyone and his brother that afternoon, because Rathe's eyelids fluttered. After struggling for a moment, they opened heavy, and the sight was glorious.

He looked up at me. "Are you an angel?"

If he thought I was an angel, something was mighty wrong.

CHAPTER TWELVE

Frailty

*E*very man for miles spoke of how Rathe must have been the luckiest man they ever knew. He cheated death by a fraction of an inch. That's how close the beams fell, grazing his clothing. Because he fell in the middle and they fell just so, he was spared, though not unscathed.

He broke his back and his left arm. The radius, the doctor called it. Along with a few assorted bumps and bruises, Rathe looked wholly out of sorts.

We took him to Creedmoor for medical attention, where he stayed for quite a while. In the weeks to follow, it felt like a small lifetime of nothing but unknowns and unrest. Luz and little Raymond cared for the homestead, and my daddy, brothers, and Jonathan took turns traveling with me back and forth, to and from Creedmoor.

Jonathan was traveling with me one particularly gusty day in early fall. I usually liked our time together, but sometimes Jonathan irked me something awful when he felt the need to talk about things that weren't his business.

"Your momma hasn't been feeling good," he dared to say.

"I know."

"You gonna visit her this weekend?"

"If I got time."

The carriage was bumpy, and I held tight to the reins, focusing on what was in front of my face rather than at the forefront of my conscience.

Jonathan pulled the collar of his jacket up to his neck and held it dear. "James's wife thinks she's heartsick. Ain't nothing outwardly wrong with her."

Sighing, I cleared my throat, which made Daddy come to mind, as that was something he did often when he was stalling to say something. But I wasn't my daddy, so I spit it out.

"If she's heartsick, it's from her own doing. I can't help her if she refuses to loose the shadows dancing around her heart when she's the one who chained them there."

He shrugged. "Maybe you can. Can't say no until you try. Can't live with anger 'cause it's easier."

"That's what I keep hearing."

Jonathan kept shifting around restlessly, adding to the bounce of our journey. "I hate to be so blunt, but what if she dies? Would you want to die like that?"

"If I live well, it don't matter how I die," I said, ending our conversation abruptly.

In another week's time, we were able to bring Rathe home for good. He was still in a lot of pain and needed all the help we could give him, but he was near enough I could check on him when my heart sped with anxiety after racing with terrible thoughts. Often, I worried that he wouldn't be able to walk right or heal well enough to work the way he always had. The way he loved to. Mostly, though, I worried the accident would change who he was on the inside. That I'd wake one day and not recognize him.

That thought scared me most of all.

Rathe suffered thoughts that scared him, too. He kept his

in, barely speaking more than necessary. I only knew because I heard him wake from his nightmares with harsh, guttural grunts, like he was falling all over again. When I would startle awake, jumping up to console him, he'd turn his head, staring at the far end of the room. So I'd tell him how much I loved him before returning to the makeshift cot I had created on the floor with spare blankets my family had given us.

And that was us. The extent of our life together for two months. It felt much, much longer. I took care of the house and animals when I wasn't busy caring for Rathe. Bathing him, reading excerpts from old back issues of *Country Life*, changing bedpans, preparing his meals, and just talking, even though he didn't respond.

I was always caring for Rathe, which meant I slept very little and didn't have time for nothing that didn't involve him or the homestead. Thankfully, we had Luz, who had picked up more sewing requests than one person was fit to handle.

Rathe receded into himself a little more each day, no matter my efforts, becoming nothing more than a lump.

One evening, while I was reading an article on blue-birds, my eyes so blurry they fought each word, I set the magazine down on my lap and stared at him. Rathe was, as usual, looking off at the far wall. All I ever saw were the wavy, matted locks on the back of his head.

"If you don't want to hear about bluebirds, tell me now. Otherwise, we're gonna be experts by the time you're done healing." I waited, but got nothing in return. "Very well then..." I took a deep breath, stretched my neck, and picked the magazine up again, continuing to read.

We had a Bible, too, but I didn't expect to make it two words in if I had to read now, being so tired. At least the magazine had pictures and large print to hold my attention.

The end of October came, and the weather was still flipping to and fro. Typical. Luz and I worked day and night, sometimes side by side; other times, passing each other in the breeze.

Caught in our never-ending loop of work, work, work, I was completely speechless when Jonathan walked through the back door one Sunday, holding something in his hand, a curious look about him.

Stacking the plates on the shelf, I asked, "Did you see a ghost or something?" When he didn't respond, yet alone move, I stopped what I was doing. "What's the matter? Are you hurt?"

Rushing over to him, he opened his mouth, but the words had crawled up inside him, refusing to come out.

He slowly held his hand out between us and turned it palm side up. When he opened his fist, I saw a frail piece of tattered material. Placing my fingers overtop, I gently unrolled it to see what it could be, exposing the delicate, once-white bird my sister Shailene had made so many years ago. The hairclip she wore every day of her life.

I gasped as tears rushed to the rims of my eyes. "Where did you get this?" I swiped it out of his hand and inspected it. Sure enough, it was Shailene's.

"Come with me," he instructed.

Forgetting to tell Rathe or Luz what I was doing, I pulled my coat off the hook and followed Jonathan out the door with purpose. We traveled a long distance by foot, until we reached the woods just past the fields I often walked in.

"This way," Jonathan said bleakly.

There were a lot of questions I wanted to ask, but my

tongue felt heavier than Barney's shiny Ford. It was near impossible to maneuver.

Just when I thought we would walk all the way to Heaven's front gate, Jonathan pointed to the left, to a swampy area where two ponds conjoined.

"Over here."

I followed him to a tree on the bank. At the base, there was a large men's boot. Looked to have been abandoned long ago. It was thick, with a mud shell.

Making sure that I could see it, Jonathan disclosed, "I found her hairclip in there."

"Inside that old boot?"

"Yeah." His gaze was downcast. "I was looking for a pond back here that's supposed to have some good fishing. I found the boot sunken down. Don't know what made me pick it up. I just... I just did, and then I saw something inside. Her clip fell out as I turned it upside down. It's been mostly protected from the weather."

"I don't understand."

"Me, either."

My brain snapped with awakening implications. I knew Shailene would never have disappeared on her own. Something had to be keeping her away. And as I looked at the dark waters of the pond, filled with the dancing reflections of the surrounding trees, I knew something foul had happened to my sister.

Throwing my coat off, I tossed it to the ground and started to walk to the edge of the pond.

"No, Nora!" Jonathan grabbed me by the arm. "She might not even be in there!"

I looked him right in the eyes. "Do you really believe that?"

He hesitated, not wanting to disagree, but unable to say yes.

"I have to see."

"No! You almost died the last time you jumped into a pond."

As serious as I'd ever been, I shook my head. "Jonathan, I ain't hopping in there without my head on my shoulders. But I'm going, and no force in this world is stopping me. Something happened to my sister, and if I can't find out what, by God, it won't be for lack of trying."

Through raggedy breaths, he let go of my arm. Nodding, he began to untie his shoes. "If you're going, I'm going," he muttered.

"You don't have to do this."

"I know," he said, "but I already got my shoes off."

Looking up at me, he smiled, and I helped him to his feet.

Wading into the water together, Jonathan admitted, "She could be anywhere. If she's even here."

"She's here," I mumbled as I searched the muck below with my toes, blindly.

Time passed as we trudged with purpose through every inch of water that didn't pass our shoulder blades. Anything past, and we were in danger of getting ourselves stuck in the mud, head below the surface. That didn't appeal to either of us.

Jonathan's teeth started to chatter. "I don't think she's here."

"She's here. We just can't reach her." Stopping to turn in every direction, I confessed, "I don't know where to look."

Not wanting to say what he was thinking, Jonathan finally conceded, "She could have settled in the middle somewhere. Erosion from the silt and mud off the banks. If so, we can't find her like this. Pond could be at least fifteen feet. Maybe more." He started wading back to the bank, but stopped and turned to me. "Somebody could have put that boot there on purpose. We ain't even certain we're looking in the right place."

Unable to admit defeat, I said, "I think I know how to find out."

We trudged to Jonathan's house first. His brother, Daryl, was leaning against the front of the house, smoking. He saw us coming and couldn't help but crinkle his nose. Covered shoulder to toe in stinking mud and other things, Jonathan carried his shoes in his hands, and I carried the strange, lone boot in mine. My coat was so sullied it about near stuck to me. We looked a sight.

When we reached the front of the house, he said, "I'd ask what you been doing, but you were with Nora so anything's possible." He tossed a rag toward Jonathan and ordered, "Take your clothes off out back. Don't wanna track mud through the whole dern house."

Jonathan stopped, asking, "Are you staying for a bit? You can change in the barn if you want. We'll scrounge up something for you to wear."

"No. I got somewhere to be."

They sensed I didn't mean home.

Daryl said, "At least change your clothes and get some shoes on first, girl. You'll get sick walking the earth like that."

"Take my horse," Jonathan offered.

I nodded. "I'll bring him back tomorrow."

It may have been wise to take Daryl's advice into consideration. Seeing as how anger was seething up inside me, though, between my organs and through my blood, I didn't listen. There was only one destination in my mind.

Riding through the cold evening, my brain circled the

details of my sister's disappearance like vultures for the picking. Through the whirling, I ended up at Momma and Daddy's in no time, having not remembered the journey at all.

"Momma!" I yelled, riding up to their house. "Momma!"

After a few seconds, Daddy lurched out the front door, gun and coat in hand. "What's the ruckus? What's happened now?"

Dismounting, I closed the short distance between us.

"I need to speak to Momma right this moment."

He took one look at the dried, stinking mud and my bare feet and muttered, "Aw, hell."

I demanded, "Momma, get out here!"

"Now hold on." Daddy held his hands out. "You gotta calm down. You can't be running crazy around here every time you get a wild hair."

Momma appeared in the doorway, her shawl draped around her. "What's going on out here? It's loud enough to wake the dead," she accused.

"Maybe that's what I'm trying to do, Momma. Ever think about that?"

I held the boot up.

"I don't understand," she confessed. "I don't know what that is."

Walking past Daddy, I dropped the boot in front of Momma and pulled Shailene's clip out of my coat pocket. "Recognize this?" I held it in front of her.

Momma yelped and ran inside.

I chased her with the strength of snake venom.

"I found it in that boot, Momma. The boot Jonathan found by a pond out past our house."

She covered her mouth in horror. I didn't know whether she was trying to hold in a scream or keep her secrets from spilling out. Either way, it looked painful, as if she would burst any moment.

"It's time." I followed her to her bedroom. "Make this right, Momma."

About collapsing on the bed, Momma sat, looking weary. "Get this girl something warm before she catches her...her death."

Daddy found a blanket and brought it in. Wrapping it around me, he said, "It's a dog blanket. You come smelling better next time, I'll pull a different blanket for you."

I made a small motion with my neck, acknowledging his words before he walked out, retiring to the living room. I sat in the high-backed chair on Momma's side of the bed and waited. And I would wait as long as it took. I wasn't going nowhere.

"I guess it's time I should tell you what I know."

"I'd say so, Momma."

CHAPTER THIRTEEN

The Footsteps of Men

*M*omma and I tucked away in the bedroom for hours as I listened to her account of Shailene, from the first troublesome moment to the last time she kissed her and said goodbye, not knowing it would be the last.

About the time Shailene stopped spending so much time with me out at the homestead, after our blessed summer of content, Momma said Shailene had befriended a young man in town. Now, he wasn't such a young man, as it turned out. Mr. Carroll was newly married at the time, getting ready to celebrate his twenty-second birthday when he first met Shailene on her way home from town.

"How you doing on such a fine day?" he had stopped to ask her.

Shailene was excited that such a handsome man was taking interest in her.

"Thankful for this beautiful day," she answered, trying not to smile too big or look too eager.

"Name's Saul." He got down from his wagon to extend a hand.

"Shailene. Good to meet you."

He kissed her hand, and she blushed.

She hadn't noticed him on that road before. Beyond that first afternoon, however, she saw Mr. Carroll quite regularly. He'd make sure to time it just so, always needing to take something somewhere. Always trying to wave or fit in a conversation.

No one knew at the time, his devoted interest in Shailene. And feeling like the brightest star in the night sky, she didn't see no harm in not telling Momma or Daddy. She also didn't realize he was hitched to another.

Feeling blessed by each day, Shailene started making arrangements to see him other times, at different places. They started meeting by her favorite pond for an afternoon dip, or along the path just before the double oaks for secret picnics. All the while, Momma thought she was out at the homestead with me, and I thought she was too busy minding her chores at home, neither of us the wiser.

It wasn't until Shailene came to Momma, worried, not knowing what to do.

"You've done walked up behind me three times in the span of one minute, child. What are you fretting over?" she had asked Shailene, knitting in her favorite chair in the living room. It was her favorite because the sun shined perfectly across her lap, illuminating her work.

Shailene swallowed hard, almost frozen with fear.

Momma stopped her work and turned around in the chair to lay eyes on her. "You look stricken, Shailene. Come, sit next to me."

She did as Momma asked, sitting on the stool beside her.

"Now," she said, taking up the knitting needles again. "What's got your tongue?"

Shailene squeaked, "Momma..."

"You're really starting to worry me. What is it?"

"Momma..."

Momma wound up her knitting needle and yarn, setting it down on the opposite side of Shailene. Turning her attention back on her daughter, she took her hands in her own. "Whatever it may be, it's better to tell me than hold it in."

Tears welled in her eyes as she crumbled, feeling safe in Momma's grasp. "I'm sorry, Momma. I'm so very sorry, to you and Daddy and God."

Preparing herself for something awful, Momma straightened her posture. "You can't be sorry to me until you tell me what you done."

"I laid with him!" she wailed. "I'm so dim, Momma. I thought he was gonna marry me. I thought he..." Her anger and humiliation poured out in an ocean of misery as Momma sat there in disbelief, still grasping her hands. Although, now she was hanging on for dear life.

"Who are you talking about, Shailene?"

"Saul Carroll. He works at his daddy's hauling company."

"You mean—"

"I thought he had feelings for me." She began to sob again. "Real feelings."

Momma felt like she couldn't catch her breath. She couldn't breathe fast or deep enough to keep up with her heart, which had shot off like a bullet.

"You and Saul Carroll laid together?"

Shailene raised her head and looked into Momma's eyes, fully transparent. Her modesty had been stolen in a moment of trickery. She had believed every sweet word he whispered her way. And when he swore up and down that he was gonna ask her daddy for permission to marry her, she never doubted his love. Only...he was giving away love that was already spoken for.

"Didn't you know Saul Carroll's married? His wife's due with their first child any day."

She shook her head vehemently. "I didn't know until today, Momma. I swear it. I didn't know." Shailene broke down again. She had cried so hard, for so long, she couldn't breathe out of her nose no more. Gasping for air like a carp, she pulled herself together enough to beg Momma, "Please don't be ashamed of me. I can't live if I know you're ashamed of me."

Leaning her head onto Momma's lap, she lost her will to cry a moment longer. Her body went slack, and she waited, still as death, for Momma to say something.

"I don't know what to think about all this, Shailene, not right now. Let me talk to your daddy."

"No!" Shailene shot up, eyes wider than a full moon. Her voice had adopted a twinge of fear. "You can't tell Daddy. I'll die. You can't tell him. Please!"

"We can't keep something like this from your daddy, Shailene. It wouldn't be right."

Going numb from a barrel of emotions, she said, barely audible, "He won't love me no more, either."

"He certainly will. Who doesn't? I'll give them a piece of my mind."

"I don't." She shook her head as it hung down. "How can I love myself if I done wrong by God? He knows. He sees everything." Slowly being overtaken by new tears, she said, "If he saw us, why didn't he warn me? Why didn't he send me a sign, Momma?"

Momma gathered her frail frame into her arms and cried with her. "I don't know."

"Why did Saul lie to me?"

"He took advantage of your trust." Momma hugged her tighter. "Some people walk around in masks, but when they take them off, they ain't no better than dirt. And a mask ain't made to last longer than its purpose."

"I don't understand how people we love can be so cruel, Momma."

"I'm sorry, my child. I truly am."

Momma rocked her for some time in her arms, tears washing their bodies.

While listening to Momma tell me her story, I could see the anguish plain as day across her face. As a mother, she hadn't seen it coming. And my momma prided herself on being watchful.

"Shailene had a secret love," I contemplated out loud.

Momma nodded. "She did. I wouldn't call it love, though. Infatuation, more like it."

"It was the only type of love Shailene ever knew, I'm sure. To go from no one noticing to somebody wanting her time."

"Well," Momma was hesitant to reveal, "she got more than his time, Nora."

"What do you mean?"

I left the chair and scooted a stool up against the side of the bed, leaning against the plush comforter. Momma pulled a blanket over her legs, figuring out how to say something so life-altering.

"Shailene fell pregnant."

"What?" I hopped up, unable to contain my surprise. "What are you talking about? Shailene never had no baby!"

Nodding adamantly, Momma groaned, "Oh, she did, Nora. She did. I'm sorry we didn't tell you, but we couldn't. We thought we were doing right by her by not speaking of it."

Momma and Daddy thought it best to send Shailene away during her pregnancy, before she was ever showing. That's why she never came home to visit, and why Momma and Daddy wouldn't take me along the few times they went to see her.

They never told Saul or his family, either.

My heart felt betrayed by the people closest to me. I could understand not letting it get out for Shailene's sake, so she could live a regular life one day. But persuading her into not telling me... Something about that struck me as unforgivable.

Feelings of resentment began to bubble to the surface. Then something peculiar happened. I remembered what Luz and Jonathan had told me: I could live my life in anger, and live hard, or I could allow myself to move past it and feel something greater. Better.

"Go ahead," Momma said, bracing herself for my wrath.

Staring at my momma, sitting on the bed a fraction of who she once was, I stood up. "Momma, there's something I need to say."

"I know, child." Shaking her head repeatedly, she forced her eyelids open. "I'm ready."

Wrapping my arms around her, cheek to cheek, I whispered in her ear, "I love you, Momma. I'm sorry."

"What?" Momma was shocked. She didn't know how to act. Maybe she expected God to come down and strike the world from existence.

I sat on the bed next to her. "I don't want to live with anger in my heart at you or Daddy. Or Shailene. That ain't no way to be." Holding her hands in mine, I looked her in the eyes. "Thank you, Momma, for telling me. Thank you for setting me free from myself."

"No," she said, "I should have told you a long time ago. It wasn't right not to. I tried to do right. I just didn't know how." Light tears ran down her cheeks. "I'm sorry you've had such torment eating away at your soul every day."

"We'll heal together, Momma."

"That sounds lovely."

We hugged once more before I walked to the door. Turning around, I had to ask, "What happened the day she disappeared?"

She shook her head, staring at the floor. "Only God knows that, Nora. I thought we had her back. My baby was home, and we were putting things right, moving on. And then..."

I nodded. "I'll work it out, Momma. I won't rest till we know."

"No! Let it rest, Nora May. Saul Carroll and his daddy got too many ties. Stay clear of them. Please."

I said, "Okay. I love you, Momma."

As I began to leave the room, Momma, in her sweetest voice, asked if I would wash my hair before bed.

"I sure will," I promised.

Passing the living room, I peeked in and said, "'Night, Daddy. See you tomorrow."

Hesitantly, he simply nodded. "Okay then."

And I did. As well as the day after that, and that. Momma's heartsickness healed in time. It took a whole heap of work on both our parts.

Retrieving Jonathan's horse that evening from the barn, I rode on home with a sort of peace in my heart for the first time in a long, long time. My sister had a whole piece of life I never knew existed. And it wasn't necessarily the secret of it that hurt. It was the pure devastation of that one piece that destroyed so many pieces for us, too. I couldn't go one day without missing Shailene something much worse than need.

If Carroll had never ridden down the road that day... If

Shailene had been sick or occupied instead... The things that might never have been could have saved us all.

But it weren't so. Everything happened, and there was no going back. All I could do was figure out a way to answer my last question: what happened to my sister the day she disappeared?

I thought on it all the way home. And when I got there, looking worse for wear, I realized that I'd run out on everyone earlier without so much as a reason or goodbye.

Walking in the back door, I saw Luz in the kitchen and immediately said, "I'm sorry for running off."

The smell of chiles rellenos and frijoles filled the entire first floor of the house. Luz turned her back to the oven. "I knew it must be for something important."

"It was. I have to wash off and check on Rathe, but I'd like to talk to you about it later if that's okay."

"Of course." She smiled and returned to the dinner, simmering and popping, ignoring my wayward attire.

When I reached the top of the stairs, I saw little Raymond in the doorway to our bedroom. He was kind of leaning against it, stepping one foot over top of the other.

"Can you tell me a story?" he asked in his cherub voice. Or, at least, that's how I imagined cherubs must sound. They should be able to melt your heart with one giggle or one word. Raymond certainly could.

Standing in the heavy rejection of silence, Raymond whispered, "That's okay."

Hanging his head lower than low, he turned and saw me at the stairs.

"I have to get cleaned up right now," I said. "But after, I don't really have much I want to do. Maybe we can tell each other some stories. I'd really like that. What do you say?"

Raymond beamed, nodding, and bounced down the steps toward his momma.

It was my turn to stand in the doorway, staring at the back of Rathe's head. My voice was a shell, but I made it count, regardless.

"I understand if you don't feel like doing much. I can't know exactly what you're going through. I know it's serious, though, to keep you down." Stepping closer, making sure Raymond hadn't snuck back upstairs, I added through gritted teeth, "But the next time that boy asks you for anything, especially something so little as your time, you better give it to him. You're the man in his life, like a daddy. I love you, and you don't need to say a word to me, but the next time you don't pay mind to that boy, I'll put you out. I swear by God."

Rustling a clean dress and undergarments out of my drawers, I took one last look at him before walking out of the room, informing him, "Now, I told my momma I'd clean my hair." And being told to clean my hair always put me in a particular mood.

The next few weeks, I continued my normal routine of caring for Rathe and the house, trying to give Luz all the time she needed to get her orders finished. And every time she got a few done, I helped wrap them up, and Raymond and I would deliver them. We made a good team, he and I. I carried the parcels, and he knocked on the doors, informing people their wait was over. Rain, snow, ice, or just raw chill —we were out there. Of course, when it was real bad, I took the wagon so Raymond could snuggle in the back under a mess of quilts my momma had made special for him.

One afternoon on our way back home, Raymond sat close at my side, bundled twice.

"Are we family?" he asked out of nowhere particular.

"Well," I started to say, "maybe not in a traditional sense, but when I look at you or when we're apart and I'm thinking about you, it feels like we're tied by that invisible string you get with family."

"Can we be?"

"You don't ever have to ask something like that. I don't know what we would have done without you or your momma. You're as close to us as family gets." I wrapped my arm around him and held the reins with the other. "I bet your momma wouldn't mind if you called us Auntie and Uncle."

His little red cheeks balled up as he smiled, nodding.

"You'll always be family, no matter how near or far we are."

"I love living with you. Momma cried a lot when we lived alone."

I squeezed him a bit tighter. "Can you even remember that far back?"

"Yep," he boasted.

"I'll tell you a secret. I cried a lot, too, sometimes, before you came to live with us. There are far less tears in the world if we stick together. Now let's get home."

"Okay."

We carried on in silent content the rest of the way home, and when we turned the bend around the corner from the house, we saw a spectacular vision.

Rathe, wearing his best winter coat, was shuffling through the front yard. His movements were rigid and downright unnatural. For not having practiced every day like he was supposed to, however, he was doing a fine job. To be honest, I'd have given him a parade just for rolling over in bed, let alone getting up and out into the world.

Luz stood by the corner of the house, keeping an eye on

him without making a fuss. When we pulled up, Raymond ran to Rathe while I walked to stand by Luz.

"When did he start doing this?" I asked, still flat astonished.

She shook her head, a look of wonder on her face.

"I don't know. I came from milking the cows ten minutes ago, no longer, and found him like this."

Pride beamed throughout my body. It warmed me like nothing had in a short eternity. Rathe was moving. He was showing some sign of life that didn't just involve breathing and blinking. There was a need to live beating inside his heart after all!

Luz was careful to remain quiet as she whispered, "I have prayed to God every day for your husband. I know I should not ask Him for specific miracles because He can only work so much good, while we must do the rest for ourselves." She turned to me, unshed tears rimming her eyes. "But God has listened, Nora. He heard my meek voice above all others and created a miracle for us."

I wasn't sure whether it was God or just Rathe's sheer will, but Luz was right. It was a miracle to see him walking about.

Raymond hopped along beside him, his mouth moving faster than a tornado, though we couldn't hear what he was saying. And although I'm sure it was a little bit of everything and then some, Rathe divided his attention between the task at hand and little Raymond's words.

I had never been prouder of my husband. There was the man who I knew still existed. That empty shell was cracking and falling away, exposing a heartbeat and a will. He was coming to life again, slowly.

Once Raymond ran over to Luz and she was able to talk

him into going inside, I decided to approach Rathe. He had made it all the way through the yard to the creek.

"Penny for your thoughts." I stood a few feet short of him. "Aunt Virgie always says that."

He tried to turn, but winced and stopped himself.

"Don't." I closed the distance between us so we could talk, if he felt like doing as much.

Rathe didn't try to move again. It seemed a chore just to stand in one place for more than a minute. His muscles were starting to tighten and complain. Couldn't blame them. They hadn't been properly used in months, having grown lazy.

"We can just stand here if you want," I said.

Not making eye contact, Rathe tenderly turned around and began to walk back to the house.

A bit of my heart crumbled, but I didn't let that stop me from feeling his accomplishment as I watched him walk all the way up to the house and disappear around the corner. It was easier to tackle one step from the back door rather than five steep ones out in front.

"That's it," I said under my breath. "You're doing it. You're coming back to me."

CHAPTER FOURTEEN

Unbearable Truths
1927

February was harsh this year. Even the mercantile had ordered an assortment of coats and shawls from Luz, asking for a speedy delivery, as winter was forecasted to travel on through the start of spring. That's how it was some years in North Carolina. Some seasons got confused, not knowing whether to thaw or freeze or just hold tight. And sometimes it did a little bit of everything in one day. Daddy always said, if you didn't like the weather, you only had to wait a few minutes. Well, Daddy couldn't take credit for that. People had been saying it for as long as he could remember.

Didn't make it any less true.

And seeing as how the clouds ruffled like a blanket of cotton through the afternoon sky, I thought it best to leave Raymond home. Jonathan accompanied me, instead. If we lost a wheel or got stuck, I'd rather have the force of a grown man than possibly place Raymond in harm's way.

"It ain't so bad," Jonathan commented.

I checked the snow. It was light and dry, which made for

easy driving, but the layer of sleet underneath promised havoc in the darker hours.

Nodding, I concluded, "We'll be fine so long as we get home before dusk."

Luz rushed out the back door, her hands full. She about tripped over her colorful skirt as it swooshed around her busy legs.

"These are the last of them." She handed me the parcels of material.

"Thank you."

"No," she beamed, telling Jonathan, "thank you for accompanying Nora so I may spend some time with my Raymond. I have been working my fingers to the bone."

"I'm sure Raymond will love that." Jonathan smiled bright.

Loading the last of the parcels and throwing a heavy blanket over them to stay dry, we hopped into the wagon and started off. The light snow was intermittent, but it still made me nervous.

I yelled behind me, "Tell Rathe I'll eat dinner with him this evening!"

"I will!" Luz yelled back.

The ride to Creedmoor was as easy as we could have wished. Nothing major occurred, and that was something to be thankful for. Of course, we couldn't say the same when we were dropping off Luz's wares.

Pulling up outside the mercantile, Jonathan threw the blanket to the side, and we got to getting. As fast as we could, we unloaded the stacks of parcels, a few at a time, taking them inside. It wasn't snowing hard yet, but we weren't taking any chances by growing lazy.

Finally, as Jonathan ran the last stack inside, a young man passed by. He looked real familiar, though I didn't know his name. His brown hat was covering his face a bit. The way he slouched, his head jutting forward, made me think of a boy from school, years ago.

As he walked on by, his gaze fell to the back of the wagon, and there was a catch in his gait. Before I could gasp, he caught himself, looking at me with the shock of a startled coyote.

"You okay?" I asked, trying to keep my own shock at bay.

"Yeah, 'course," he barked, picking up the pace and vanishing around the corner.

He had been heading straight for the mercantile, but changed at the last minute, after his blunder.

When I turned around to see what had caught his attention, I saw the boot. It was *the* boot that Jonathan had found by the pond with Shailene's hairclip.

Immediately, my heart skipped a couple of necessary beats as I leapt from the seat to run around the corner. I watched intently as the boy picked up his pace, aiming for the post office.

Swiftly, I ran from one obstruction to the next, trying to keep out of his focus.

At last, I came around the side of a tree, peering past to the young stranger as he approached a man with a lot of thick facial hair. It was hard to see who he was. So many men grew beards and mustaches to keep themselves warm during the cold months.

Daring a bit closer, I ducked behind a dirty Ford truck. It was stuck in the snow, obviously not going nowhere anytime soon. There was a distinct smell of petrol mixed in with the overly ripe snow air. My nose crinkled as I tried not to get distracted by it.

Upon further study, I realized the bearded man was Saul Carroll.

An unfamiliar feeling ripped up through my gut. It was telling me to feed him to the mountain lions and listen to him scream for mercy. It wanted me to scold him in front of his whole family, so his wife could see what a deviant she was tied down to for all eternity. So his children could look upon the monster under his mask and scream until their eyes popped out of their little heads.

As I watched, Saul reacted with conviction. I saw him raising his voice at the young man, wishing I could hear past the crunching of snow every which way, along with people carrying on with chores, all trying to get done and get home.

There was definite anger in the way he squinted his eyes and tightened his lips. Something was awry. I wanted so badly to confront him, the man who robbed my sister of her purity and happiness with ugly lies.

Shailene was gone. I didn't know how yet, but I could spit on a bull's eye as to why. And it stood in front of me, yelling at somebody else for his own evil deeds.

"What are you doing?" Jonathan whispered, sneaking up behind me.

"Holy Ghost!" I about yelled, covering my own mouth before it escaped into the open world.

"I thought you'd be waiting with the wagon."

"I was," I returned. "And then I wasn't." Pointing, I said, "Look at that man. Guess who he is?"

He froze, knowing all too well who Saul Carroll was. Only one of the most spoiled grown men for five counties.

"What are you doing eavesdropping on Carroll? Let's get on out of here before he spots us."

"And what'll he do then, Jonathan? Have us arrested for knowing what he did?"

"Nora..." Jonathan tried to be gentle when he said, shaking his head, "We don't know a dern thing about what he did, save what your momma told you. And that's only going on hearsay from Shailene."

In a threatening tone, I informed him, "If you're calling my family liars, we're gonna have more than words, Jonathan."

"I ain't. I just mean that nobody knows what happened to her when she up and didn't come home. What if she really did drown by accident? What if something else, altogether, is to blame? You can't damn a man for simply breathing wrong."

"Listen to me. I've known from the day they sent her away, to the day she came back, to the day I lost her last that an evil ascended on my poor sister. Now, if Saul Carroll didn't do it himself, that boy sure enough helped. Just look at him! The fear of God has got a hold on him."

We stopped arguing long enough to scrutinize the young stranger's demeanor once more.

"See?" I nudged. "He's plum petrified of Carroll. That man's got something over on him. They both know it, and so do I." Pleading with pain and suspicion in my eyes, I asked Jonathan, "Can you tell me different?"

"Damn it!" he cursed to himself. "I believe you, all right? Now let's get outta here. The snow's getting ready to fall again. We can talk about it on the way home."

"All right," I surrendered.

Sneaking along, back to the edge of the mercantile, we linked arms over a particularly icy lane and fell on our behinds. It was something of a debacle, taking us a few exaggerated minutes to stand our ground and cross to safer footing.

When I looked back, however, I saw Carroll standing still as a scarecrow, staring.

"Shoot, he sees us," Jonathan said under his breath. "Act regular. Get in the wagon."

Without skipping a beat, I disappeared around the corner to the front of the store. We hopped up and hauled outta town faster than a goose at Christmas.

Once we were on our way, safely outside of town, we slowed the horses.

Muttering, I confided to Jonathan, "I'm going to find out that man's truth."

"I know you are. That's what scares me, Nora."

The snow started to come down thick, in large flakes.

"Scare you? If you're scared by the truth, you might as well live life covering your eyes with a pillow."

"I'm scared he's gonna send you to find your sister."

He was frightened that Saul Carroll was going to put me with my sister, silenced for the everlasting journey. Not knowing how to respond, I stayed silent the rest of the way back to the homestead.

Jonathan and I didn't say nothing to anyone at home. There wasn't much to say, really, that wouldn't stir more fear and concern, so we let it be. For safe measure, though, I took that old boot, wrapped it in a spare piece of cloth, and hid it under the house. I wasn't sure why. It just seemed the smartest course of action at the moment, considering.

I couldn't bring myself to do the same to Shailene's prized hairclip. That little white bird spoke to a part of my soul like nothing else could anymore. I perched it on top of our dresser drawers, leaning it against the small wood box Rathe kept his daddy's pipe in. The pipe was more of a keepsake. So was the hairclip. It only seemed natural they might find a small space in time together, reminding us that ghosts come in many forms.

A few weeks passed, and Jonathan and I still refused to

speak of the event in town. My mind kept mulling it over and over. *How could I drag his sin to light?* Carroll's family had too much money to stay honest, and too many notable acquaintances to be accountable.

Turned out, I was overthinking it all. Leave a devil to play, he'll come knocking soon enough.

CHAPTER FIFTEEN

The Devil's Doorstep
1927

*M*arch 1, 1927 was a doozy of a snowstorm. Jonathan's brother, Daryl, was real sick. Colin was away with Dorthea, visiting her family in Virginia. Jonathan didn't know what to do, so the night before, he'd come to our house, looking for answers.

Luz brewed a special tea for him to take home, but it didn't seem to be settling Daryl's cough any. And by the following morning, their porch collapsed under the pressure of the ice on the roof, dumping the last of their wood pile right down an incline into the snow.

We had plenty to spare. Hooking the wagon up to the horses, Jonathan, Luz, and I loaded it with enough wood to keep them warm, but not enough to get Jonathan stuck on his way home.

"I'll go with you, check on Daryl myself," I informed him.

"It will be too dangerous to come back on your own. I'll go with you," Luz voiced.

My head practically vibrated, it shook so much. "Can't. Rathe ain't in a place to watch the little one on his own yet."

Luz was visibly disappointed, but she couldn't argue the truth.

Jonathan hated to agree, but he didn't want me to find myself in a bad way. He shook his head, over and over, finally saying, "No. If something ever happened to you, Nora, Daryl and me would feel forever responsible. You're like a sister to us. You're family. We can't have nothing happen to you."

"Let us ask Rathe," Luz suggested.

I balked. "Don't you dare! He's been milling about like the dead for months with nothing to say. He ain't about to get a vote right now." Looking straight into Jonathan's eyes, I said, "I'm going. Get in the wagon."

He knew by my tone that I wasn't to be reasoned with. Luz knew, too, though she tried her best, regardless.

Finally, after I was wrapped in layer upon layer with my boots, scarves, hat, and gloves, she gave in, handing us each a quilt and a cup of hot cocoa to tide us over during the ride. I hugged her tight one last time before heading out.

"I won't be gone long. I'm not staying."

Jonathan instructed Luz, "If she ain't back by four, shoot the rifle once. I'll go looking."

She nodded, hoping that wouldn't be the case.

"I'll be back," I reassured her from the bench as the horses started their slow trek.

It was more of a struggle to get there than I had anticipated, even considering the weather. We persisted on, though. I know I quietly thanked every bit of earthly fabric when we turned the bend and saw the smoke from Jonathan's house trailing the sky. We looked at each other and just nodded, both breathing freer.

Soon as we got there, I checked on Daryl and helped unload the wood into the dry cover of the barn. Their porch needed work something awful, but at least the roof hadn't torn a hole in the siding when it gave. It went clean and quick.

Hugging me, Jonathan said, "Okay, get going."

The snow was packed tight against the earth. It was almost a foot deep and growing. We hadn't had a snow like this in some time, especially not in March. The whole state was getting buried faster than we could dig.

"Get inside!" I yelled from the wagon. "Keep Daryl warm!" Waving, I pulled out, taking it nice and slow. I won't lie; I had to remind myself more often than not to breathe. Between the cold and the sheer silence around me, like the world had fallen into a deep sleep, my nerves were bouncing all through my body.

I had made it halfway home when, all of a sudden, the wagon shuddered and the horses jarred to a stop.

"What's going on?" I asked the horses.

Working in the confinement of my clothing layers, I awkwardly climbed down, fighting the snow to see what the problem was.

"Now how'd those get there?" I said under my breath.

There were three gigantic rocks the size of my head in the middle of the road. One had caught the wheel, causing it to pull the horses to a violent halt. We had come the same way before, and I hadn't remembered anything being there. It was very well, we could have simply missed them by a few inches and been none the wiser.

"Dern it!"

I got down on my knees, lifting it with all the might in my back, rolling it just enough to the side to clear the wheels for a second attempt. "That's it," I mused. "We did it." I looked up, smiling at the horses. "Let's get back."

As I stood, fighting the pull of the thick snow, a shot rang out in the distance, startling the horses. They bucked and took off. The wagon, being empty, didn't weigh nothing, allowing them to cut through the snow like butter. Only problem was, they'd left me behind.

"Wait!" I called out. "Brownie, wait!"

Being halfway home, I decided to trudge onward, wondering who the lone shot had come from. I knew Luz and Jonathan wouldn't mistake it as our communication. I hadn't been given enough time to make it home yet. Still, I walked as fast as my legs would grant me.

The silence was nearly deafening. After a bit, a soft *shhhh* filled the world—partly the wind, partly the light dusting of snow gliding across the hardened snow already spread across the land. I wasn't sure which was worse, the silence or the *shhhh*.

An occasional limb would snap, ringing out every which way, though the world refused to wake.

My toes were growing colder as the chill from the ground ate at the soles of my boots. Frost covered my gloves, trying to smother the warmth inside. And worry wormed a path into my brain.

Another snap rang out. I was loath to seek out the culprit branch, but I made myself look over my shoulder. If, for any reason, to keep moving every part of me I could.

When I turned my neck, glancing off the road behind me, something dark caught my eye. Reeling, I turned and stopped, listening. The gentle *shhhh* persisted.

"Come out! I saw you!" I yelled, paranoid.

About the time I was getting ready to turn back, a figure stepped out from behind a great oak, his dark coat blotting the landscape like a boil.

The man with the beard.

Saul Carroll.

I wanted to run. Scream like the world was on fire.

Holding my composure, I asked, "What are you doing out here?"

He didn't answer.

"You lost?" I tried again.

Shhhh.

Turning around, I started to walk briskly. The weight of my layers began to pull on my legs, causing the muscles in my thighs to burn. I counted my breaths, trying to keep them steady so I wouldn't hyperventilate.

Out. One, two, three, four.

In. One, two, three, four.

Out. One, two, three, four.

I dared to look back. Carroll stood in the middle of the road, a lot dern closer than he'd been a few minutes ago.

"What do you want?" I asked, continuing to walk.

As if he could read my frantic thoughts about screaming, he spoke smooth and low. "I want to talk."

Walking a bit faster, I spoke loudly, saying, "It ain't a day for talking. Don't you see all the snow? It's dangerous out."

"It's an ideal day to talk," he answered.

I didn't know what he meant by that, but something deep inside was telling me I didn't want to find out.

Keeping track of my whereabouts, I had surmised that the cleared tobacco fields I walked in so often were just on the other side of the tree line. If I could get past the brush fast enough, I might have a clear shot to the house through the field. It was still a ways, though. A lot could go wrong in that time.

Counting my breathing again, I bided my time, listening as he grew a bit closer.

In. One, two, three.

Out. One, two, three.

In. One, two, three.

Out. One—

I took off, bounding through the snow, off the road, toward the trees.

"Damn it!" he cursed.

The snow squeaked and crunched so loud, I couldn't separate the sound of his footsteps from mine. Unable to know how close he'd come, I forced my legs to perform like they'd grown hooves and extra muscles. I had never run so hard in my life. Something felt ill inside my chest, or broken, rattling around my stomach. My body was trying to tell me to stop, but my brain kept screaming until it turned into a roar.

I listened to my brain.

It wasn't till I reached the middle of the empty field that I felt his hand come down on my shoulder, tumbling us both to the ground.

My muscles wanted to seize. My heart wanted to turn to mush and melt right into the snow. But I got to my feet just as he grabbed me again.

"What are you doing?" I screamed.

He dropped me to the ground and sat on top of me.

"Where'd you get that boot?" he demanded.

I spit in his face. "Get off me!"

He slapped me across the mouth. When I refused to show pain, he slapped me again, this time coming down across my right eye.

"Where'd you get the boot?"

Struggling, I bucked him a few times, making him lose his balance. He gained it back, though, at the last minute. Grabbing me by the collar of my coat, he lifted my shoulders to him and screamed in my face, "Where?" until his voice nearly gave out.

Glaring at him, I snarled, "You know where."

He slapped me a few times more, back and forth, from one side of my face to the other, until I started to feel nauseous. Letting out a raspy grunt each time, he hit with speed and strength. When he was finished, he lowered my shoulders and head down into the snow, and the reach of the cold crept in.

We fell quiet for a moment. He was trying to gauge what kind of a threat I'd be. I was trying to think of something I could use as a weapon. When nothing else came to mind, I drew my knee up sharp, right between his legs.

He buckled, and I took the moment to pull my hand into a fist and hit him right in his temple. I leapt to my feet as he swooned, but he grabbed my ankle, tripping me down again.

When I flipped to my back, he had stood up, towering above me. I could see it then. His true face.

"I see your sin," I managed to say with a rapidly swelling lip.

He froze, as if looking at a ghost. "What?"

"You can't hide it now. I see your sin."

"How?" His voice stumbled. "How could you know?"

I could tell something had spooked him awful.

"That you killed my sister?"

He shook his head frantically. "Those were the last words she spoke to me... 'I see your sin.'"

I hadn't known any of that, actually. And if he could read minds, he would have known there wasn't much in my cupboard that I *did* know about him.

"What did you do to my sister?"

"Nothing."

I screamed, "Liar!"

"It wasn't me." His voice cracked. "It wasn't me. I didn't do it."

"The man I saw you with in town..."

Carroll nodded, hesitant to say it out loud. I wasn't sure whether he felt bad because Shailene was dead or because he didn't have the stomach to do it himself.

"He was just a school boy when I hired him to...take care of your sister. He and his friends needed money to feed their families. Hunger will make a young man do questionble things, Mrs. Cravis." A shadow of something I couldn't place passed his expression. "Shailene was sweet and caring and genuine, but she wouldn't let go. And the need... God, the need I had for her was stifling." He sighed. "She was too young and pure to understand. I was married, for gall sakes."

Listening to Carroll confess should have felt better. Righting God's truth somehow. Instead, I was watching a man start to cry, telling me how much he loved my sister. Under the light of day, I started to cry, wondering how such a horror could come about out of such love.

"Why didn't you just let her be?" I asked, near pleading.

"I did, damn it! Then she left. I thought it was her way of moving on. It was over. Done."

"But she left to—"

"To have our baby."

Searching his face, I tried to figure out how he found out about her being pregnant.

"She told me," he confessed. "I hadn't seen her in well over a year. Then, just like the first day all over again, I passed her on the road, hauling."

"You didn't have to stop." I sat up, my legs pulled together in front of me.

"No, I didn't." Carroll almost sounded beat.

"But you did," I accused.

"I did. Just like the first day, I... I couldn't help myself."

"You're a weak man."

"From your mouth to God's ear." He dropped to his knees in front of me, a tear streaming down his cheek. "I kissed her. And right there in the road, she told me everything."

My voice felt limp as I asked, "Why did you steal her from us?"

"Because she would have told. Sooner. Later. Didn't matter. I knew then I wouldn't be able to stay away from her."

I broke down in tears. "You're a thief. You're the worst kind of thief. And a coward. You couldn't let them see who you really are, to be accountable for your sins," I sobbed.

"I didn't kill her."

"Keep saying that all you want. It won't make it true. It won't bring her back to me."

"I wasn't the one who... They did that, not me." He shook his head almost violently. "Not me."

"Because of you!" My teeth clenched. "They were children. They looked to you, and you made them think killing one of their own was all right. And that's what she was, a child. She wasn't supposed to be your mistress. She wasn't supposed to be a mother. She wasn't supposed to bear all of those secrets that rotted everything away."

He bowed his head. "I'm so tired."

"The wicked don't need sleep." Staring him down, I said, "You got one more question to answer. Why'd my daddy find Shailene's pack and shoe?"

Almost cocky, he spat, "'Cause I told that boy to go far from where he left her and make it look like an accident." Gathering a renewed sense of hostility, he pulled a pocket knife out of his jacket. "I can't bring her back, and that is regrettable. I do, however, plan on giving you two a family reunion."

Something about him turned off. The lilt in his tone disappeared, and he didn't seem to care about what he planned to do to me.

I shook my head. "That ain't gonna happen."

As if the world resigned, he suddenly tried to pounce. In that short while, I managed to raise my leg and catch him in his chest. Using every haunting moment without Shailene, every shed tear, every soundless scream that had tortured me, I shoved him backward with a might that couldn't have been my own doing. In an instant, I was on my feet, cold as they were, readying myself into a stance, waiting for him to spring to his feet.

He never did.

Hesitantly, I shuffled wide around his fallen form, close enough to take a look.

Wheezing, he laid awkwardly on his back, his right leg jutting out to his side. It moved back and forth in a gawky manner, like someone had it on puppet strings. His lips were moving along, though it took a full minute for his words to catch up.

Breathing heavily, he was able to say, "Something... My back..."

I moved the snow out of the way around him to find cut tobacco stalks spearing from the ground. Carroll must have landed right on a frozen shoot about four inches tall. Falling with the strength of my kick combined with his weight, it pierced his back something terrible, pinning him to the ground.

"Get help..." he tried to say over and over.

My heart thumped about, rushing beats, skipping beats,

until I felt flush. Squatting, I placed a gloved hand in the snow in front of me for balance.

"What if I can't?" I asked.

Unable to form a complex sentence, his brows scrunched as confusion set in.

"Why?" he finally puffed.

Still crouched, I asked, "What if this should be your end?"

His eyes turned bulbous, alarm screeching through his being. Shaking his head, he mouthed, "No."

I nodded in return, hugging my knees to my chest, not three feet from his misery.

"I don't want to kill you," I admitted. "But I can't save you."

Carroll made an uncontrollable whistling noise from his throat.

"I'm sure someone had a chance to do right by my sister. I'm positive that moment passed by without doubt. I've given it thought, if that's a consolation. Like I said, I can't do you harm on purpose, but I can't leap in the path of fate, either."

Something like a, "Ha, ha," came out of his mouth, though it was far from a laugh. He was trying to speak.

"Save your energy," I recommended. "I won't be giving your family any last words."

He would be eaten up into God's graceful world as if He called him home, body and soul. Nothing left but an empty grave, like my Shailene.

I waited, squatted beside him so he wouldn't have to die alone. After a while, the cold became a comfort. It let me know I was still alive. And as much as I despised myself in that moment for not harboring enough love in my heart for a fellow creature, the cold let me know that I'd rather it be him than me fighting for that last breath.

Would it change anything, knowing Shailene's fate? I wasn't sure. No answers came with the slow, quiet death of Saul Carroll in the empty tobacco field on the impossible day the world slept.

Ninety pounds can sink any man.

Indeed, they had.

For my sister.

I heard Jonathan's rasp tenor call across the field, "Nora, is that you!"

How was I supposed to explain such a vulgar sight? How was I? Quickly, I realized there were no justifications strong enough, so I never tried.

He ran through the thickening snow, reaching us far faster than I'd thought him capable of doing. Not that I was doing much thinking in that moment.

Stopping abruptly, he stared at Carroll's limp, distorted body. He was carrying a pistol with him. His family didn't own pistols, only rifles for hunting.

"Where'd you get that?" I asked.

Catching his breath, he said, "I found it right off the road. Lucky to have seen it. It was practically buried in all this snow." His eyes shifting from the body to me and back, he asked gently, "Want to talk about what happened?"

"Not even if I were standing in front of Hell's gates," I confessed.

He shrugged. "All right."

Silently, Jonathan picked up Carroll's legs.

"What are you doing?" I asked, soberly.

"Not me, we. We're gonna dump him in the pond just down the road. It's no less than twenty feet in the middle. Real good drop-off on the edges, too."

I shook my head. "We're gonna leave him where he lays."

"But he'll be out in the open for somebody to find."

"Not before the coyotes get to him. And not before all this snow melts. Won't be nothing left but an unlucky man who fell just right."

Jonathan whipped the pistol out of the back of his pants and shoved it between Carroll's belt and pants. "There."

"Maybe he was out hunting. Or got lost in a white storm."

The shaking was starting to set in something terrible.

"Come on," Jonathan requested, wrapping his arm around me. "I caught up with the horses before I knew you'd left the road and made your own path. They're waiting past the trees."

He was trying to act normal, but I could hear the change. Jonathan was shaken. Could be, he didn't like seeing a dead body. Could be, my ability to sink a man scared him. Or maybe he didn't care for one dang bit of it because he was a decent man.

We made it back to his house, by the grace of somebody watching over us that day. I don't think it was God. If He is up there, I don't think He'd sit around watching me watch a man die.

The snowfall from the mighty storm broke records. It left every city around incapacitated. We got well over two feet, and one hell of a memory that would burn nightmares like they were daffodils in a drought.

The following day, I cleaned up the cuts and lumps on my face as best I could and bee-lined straight to Momma and Daddy's. Shailene would have been buried in the family plot on the hill, where her headstone stood, and I intended to hold true to the words I had spoken so long ago to Momma.

I won't visit that damn stone until I discover what horrible evil befell my sister, even if it means never setting eyes on her grave.

Jonathan and I rode up on Brownie. Getting down, I went for a shovel in the barn as he took Brownie in, out of the cold.

I didn't hesitate, making my way up the small hill. Standing at the modest iron gate, I searched the headstones. There were grandparents, cousins, uncles. And my dear Shailene.

Using the shovel, it didn't take long to clear layers of snow and ice. I brushed the headstone clear with my gloves. And as I swept the base, I found a stone lamb sitting peacefully, sleeping. That's all it took, making a flood of every emotion from the last seven years come out all at once, fighting for the right to live in the light of day.

I crumpled to the ground and sobbed like I'd never sobbed before. It was violent and raw and loud, causing my throat to sting, my ears to throb. And there didn't seem to be no end. When one wave would settle, I'd only have enough time to catch my breath before another would possess me.

When my tears finally dried up, I pounded my fists against the stone that rested under the lamb. I wanted to do more, to turn into a great horse and cause a stampede, or scar the earth in pockmarks. Feeling destructive, I was suddenly reminded of Shailene's extreme tenderness.

I love birds. If we were birds together, we could fly across land and sea... I wish I could be a bird more than anything sometimes.

I was such a creature of dirt and earth, and she was always soaring above, never wanting her feet to leave the clouds.

Kissing my hand, I touched it to the stone. "Not a day without you. Not one."

Wiping my tears, I grabbed the shovel and stood up,

heading down the hill. Along the way, I saw Daddy holding Momma by the arm. There was shock plain as day when they saw my face, busted and raw. Bruises had sprouted along my cheekbones, and the right side of my mouth was cracked, swollen three times larger than its usual proportions.

As I approached them, Daddy cleared his throat. "Are the angels singing her song?"

They remembered my promise, as well. I think a part of them never wanted to see me at that grave because it gave them a tiny piece of hope that Shailene was still blessing the world with her laughter somewhere, lighting someone's way like she'd done for us.

But it wasn't so. Her light shined somewhere else now. Maybe somewhere in the clouds. I liked to think of her as the star I wished on every night.

I nodded to Daddy, unable to bring myself to say it out loud.

Momma wailed. She sounded feral, howling as a wounded predator might be likened to do, and nearly collapsed in Daddy's arms as tears ran down both of their faces. It was the first time I ever remembered seeing my daddy cry. Really cry. I wasn't sure what to do. They didn't need me; they needed Shailene. For so many reasons, I'd never understand why Shailene, the kindest thing around, got cheated out of something as glorious as life.

Passing by as they trudged up the hill in a ton of snow, I said, "It's finished, Daddy."

It didn't take long to put the shovel away and head home with Jonathan. When Brownie came to a full stop at the homestead, I put her away for the evening, out of the cold.

Walking through the back door, I saw Jonathan sitting at

the little table, playing with Raymond. Luz met me at the door. I'd been gone since the afternoon before.

"I heard Jonathan's shot yesterday. I thought it meant you were to stay with them, that the weather was too much." Inspecting my beaten appearance, she looked from me to Jonathan and back again. Shaken, she exclaimed, "I see I was wrong."

Turning my head sideways, shielding my bruises from Raymond, I asked, "Can you check on Uncle Rathe for me? I got something I need to speak to your momma about."

"Yes," he answered, having jumped from his seat, practically to the top of the stairs already.

"Thanks!"

Luz sat at the table, and we carried on an entire conversation in whispers and hushed tones.

"How do you feel about it?" Luz asked, after thinking for a few moments.

I shrugged. "I don't know. I expect it'll always change in my heart, feeling different as I age and grow my knowledge. It felt right, sitting there, watching him. It might not feel so right a few years from now, or when I'm old and have a kinder heart." Shrugging, I said, "But I did it, and I'll have to accept it through every rung of my life."

I didn't say no more about it, not ever, though I knew that day would be part of me forever. It would never fade or tarnish with age. I'd never be free of Saul Carroll's pleading voice echoing in my head. Or the expression of reluctance, even then, in a moment of pure honesty, to accept the price of his choices. But my sister, wherever she was, body and spirit, was free of him. I'd carry his weight as long as it kept him from sinking her for eternity.

CHAPTER SIXTEEN

Revival

*A*s the birds took to the skies, chirping and fluttering about with more gumption, alerting us to the warming weather, I often found myself sitting on the porch swing or walking the creek rather than the tobacco field. I stayed away from it with a furious knowledge of what we could be.

Rathe had been walking more often on his own with less trouble, without me goading him to keep practicing. He had even started saying small things like "please" and "more." It was a sight to have him back at the dinner table with us. Luz and I beamed as we watched Raymond practically hop out of his skin with excitement.

There'd been a distinct change in Rathe when I came back from that field, beaten and, moreover, altered from my heart to the back recesses of my brain. Something awakened. He started to do small things in the beginning, like feeding the pigs or grooming the horses. We didn't know how to react at first. Should we applaud his efforts or ignore them and let him be? It was hard feeling like a stranger to my own husband, not knowing how to act. Wondering whether he'd respond with resentment or delight.

Watching him tend to a fractured board by the horses, I spoke my mind with Luz.

"I don't know what to think."

"It does not please you to see him so alive?"

Scrubbing the dishes, I shook my head. "Of course! I ain't saying nothing of the sort. It's just...he's practically been a ghost. I've got all these feelings mixed up inside. I've been so angry at him for letting go so easy. And then come these feelings of compassion, because I can't understand everything he's feeling. It ain't fair to damn him for that." Luz moved to stand beside me, placing her hand across my shoulder as I confessed, "But a part of me wants to."

"He is still the same man. He is your husband."

"I feel like you're more of a husband than he's been. You and I are the ones working to the bone, scrounging to sell anything we could spare. Milk, pies, blankets, shirts." Motioning between us, I continued, "We're the ones who have sat at this table, making ends meet any which way, eating beans and cabbage every other day."

Grabbing my chin with her hand, she pulled me forward, locking our lips together. Unable to fully react, I just stood there, feeling the pressure of her soft lips across mine. Time seemed to turn its back on us, and I could have sworn the dish water was growing cold.

When Luz withdrew, she brushed my hair behind my ears. "What are your feelings now?"

I stumbled over my words, eventually gaining my footing.

Shrugging, I confessed, "It should have felt like love had come down in the form of an angel to carry me to safety, but...it didn't feel like that."

Luz smiled, pleased. Tsk-tsking her head back and forth,

she said, "Because I am not your lover. He is out there," she pointed, "fixing your fence."

We laughed together as she hugged me.

It was her turn to admit, "You are the dearest friend I have ever had. As friends, we will always be as one when there is a need. When we work our hands to the bone to eat and survive, we stand together, as one, because I have a great love for you, and you for me. But it is not the same as the love you and Rathe share. It is not passion." Picking up the last dish and scrubbing it, Luz said, "I thank God for you and Rathe every day, for giving my Raymond and me such love."

Looking out the window, I muttered, "I don't know if I believe in God anymore."

Luz shrugged. "Love those around you well and be thankful for life. That is all you need to do. If there is God, He will see the good in you. If there is not, life is still worth treating as a gift."

Laughing, I asked, "How'd you get so wise? I'm bumping my head into doorframes in the dark most of the time, trying to come up with one complete thought."

She smiled. I picked up a cloth and began drying the dishes.

"We learn in our own time," was all she said. "My mother used to always say this when she was living."

"When did she pass away?"

I didn't know if I should have asked or not, but I stood by my decision and waited for her reply.

"Two weeks before my daughter. My village was overwhelmed with the sickness."

"I'm so sorry," was all I could think to say, though I meant it all the way to the spine of my soul.

"It is my path to walk. They helped to make it."

"What if you make your own path?"

"Then... Then maybe you are set apart from the rest of us, that being both difficult and freeing."

Thinking on her statement, I agreed.

"Rathe is still outside. Maybe you should speak to him."

"I think I should," I agreed.

As I walked out the back door, I found Rathe fiddling with something at the edge of the yard, close to the wild-flower patch I took such pride in.

Walking up behind him, I asked, "What are you doing?"

When he turned around, I could see a tiny wooden box on a pole.

"I thought your flowers could use some friends."

"Well, what is it?" Fighting a smile, I subdued my curiosity, waiting for him to answer before I started guessing.

"It's a bluebird house." When I kept quiet, he added, "It has to face east. That's what the articles mentioned, right?"

I nodded.

"Time of year is right. If I get this up, we might have bluebirds this year."

I was in absolute shock. This was more than Rathe had said altogether in the last six months.

"Why?"

Dropping his tools, he walked slowly over to me and took my hands in his. Kissing my palms, he smiled. "'Cause I always want you coming home to me."

I slid my hands out from his and clasped them against his cheeks. Wanting to cry with joy, I planted the longest kiss on his lips instead. And in that moment, I felt the warmth of beating angels' wings surrounding us with a feverish tornado of affection. When I finally let him go, he wrapped me in his arms, resting his right cheek on top of my head.

He spoke low and true. "I was listening to every word. Each day, as you tried calling me back from that hell, I listened. Just weren't able to act on it until now."

Sinking against his chest, I breathed a heavy sigh of relief. Tears rimmed my eyes, but I refused to give them their due. This was my day. It was a waking portrayal of every night's dream since Rathe had been stricken, and I intended to bask in every precious second of it.

There was no going back to silent meals or one-ended conversations. Rathe would be facing the world, starting with his family.

The man standing in front of me was familiar. He worked hard, no matter the undertaking, and loved with such a light it challenged the sun.

"Why has it taken so long?"

His gaze dropped to the ground. "I just felt like I wasn't whole. I couldn't understand how I was supposed to take care of you when I couldn't even bathe myself. You don't know what that's like for a man. I made a promise to your daddy that I wouldn't leave you to the four winds. It didn't make sense in my mind, how that wouldn't happen, given my state."

Raising my eyebrows, I pursed my lips. "So all this was because you were afraid to let my daddy down?"

"No!" he balked. "I mean, a little."

"Then, Rathe Cravis, don't you stand here after six months of nothing and tell me half-truths."

He grunted, pacing back and forth the best he could. Although he had been practicing, there was still progress to be made. He had to be mindful not to move too quickly or turn too sudden. As he paced, I could see him tugging his pants back up to his waist. Rathe had lost some weight, or rather some muscle, while he was bedbound. It'd come back, though, once he started caring for himself again and working little by little.

"And why, by God, don't you just put on a pair of suspenders?"

He stopped pacing and, looking out of the corners of his eyes, trying to hold a smile at bay, said, "Because it hurts to reach over my shoulders. I can't clip 'em, neither."

"Then why don't you just ask for help?" I approached him, wrapping my arms around his waist, trying not to laugh.

"That'd be too easy, I guess."

"We've made it this far, Rathe. A pair of dern suspenders ain't nothing."

Rathe shook his head as it hung low, the humor having disappeared.

Looking up into his face, I asked, "What's really wrong?"

He tried to turn away, but I pulled him back, not letting him go so easy this time.

"What happened?"

It took him a few tries before he finally said, "I didn't think you could love me anymore. Not like that. You had to care for me more like you would a child. I couldn't work or even walk to the bathhouse. Asking you to see me as the man you married, well, that was impossible. Hell, I didn't even recognize myself."

"Do you know what makes a man attractive?"

"His ability to take care of his family," Rathe answered with conviction.

Twisting the shirt material at his sides in my fists, I corrected, "Devotion. That's the most attractive part of a man."

"I don't understand."

Of course he didn't. All he'd ever heard growing up was

how to build a homestead and grow a farm and protect his family. He didn't know anything about a woman's heart. It could have been a cow dancing on a horse, and he would have just walked by, scratching his head, going, "Huh."

"When you focus on getting well, like you are now, so we can be whole again, together...that's devotion. When you're fixing that board over by the horses, even while your back is screaming in agony, but you know it's gotta get done, that's devotion. There's nothing stronger, because that's pure love. That's what's going to keep me coming home to you for the rest of our lives."

He hugged me as if I were a wild creature about to escape his grasp.

"I'm sorry I've been so dense."

And that was the beginning of our second love. People are complex, that's for sure. When we're growing and trans- forming, we have to remember to do it together. And when we do, sometimes a new type of love blossoms, stealing our breath with kisses sent from angels.

My heart healed more every given day. But it wasn't set right until Momma fell ill again. This time, no one expected her to recover.

CHAPTER SEVENTEEN

Home Again

"*M*omma?" I knocked on her bedroom door.
"Come on in."

I pushed the door open slowly. Momma was tucked under a thick comforter, only her arms and head free.

"Hi, Momma."

She grumbled, her brow furrowing. "Why can't you wear something other than riding pants?"

Looking down at my dusty pants, I shrugged. "They nearly look like a skirt if I move just so." Swishing my legs back and forth, I felt justified. "See?"

Giving me a weary expression, she motioned with her hand. "Come over here. Sit by me."

I pulled up the high-backed chair until one of the armrests cozied against the bed. "Daddy said you hadn't left this dern room in nearly a week. Is that true?"

"He don't have no right talking about my personal business. And what if it is? It's my right. I can die wherever I like."

"Momma." I gasped. "You're not dying! You caught a bug, is all. Daddy had it. Dewey had it. Holy Ghost, Momma, even James came over and got it. And we all know, if the

Beyond is calling, they might as well take James first. They wait much longer, he'll be too ornery to walk through the pearly gates."

She chuckled at that. "Now don't talk about your brother that way, Nora." Her words didn't hold water. She laughed some more until she needed a tissue for the edges of her eyes.

A terrible idea burrowed into my brain, and I couldn't stop myself before it barreled right outta my mouth.

"What if you spend some time with me at the homestead?"

Momma perked up. "I don't understand. You're asking me to pack a bag and leave your daddy?"

"Well, not like that. Just for a week or two. We can get some canning done, and some shucking. My wildflowers are so pretty right now. And there's a whole family of bluebirds waiting to hatch." Wondering whether I should mention it, I added softly, "I can show you Shailene's favorite fishing spot in the creek."

"No one could possibly do any fishing in that shallow thing."

She said one thing, but I could see her thoughts turning to Shailene.

"It was just her spot for watching the minnows swim back and forth. Wasn't no real fishing. Shailene never wanted to hurt the fish."

"Sounds like Shailene."

There was a knock at the door.

"Oh, I forgot. I brought someone else to see you. Eula!"

"Oh," Momma tsk-tsked. "Here we go again. You girls will fight anywhere, even on my deathbed."

"No, Momma, it ain't like that. There'll be no screaming today."

"And what makes you promise that?"

"Because little ears don't need to hear such nonsense."

Eula walked in, big as the moon. Her belly looked like it had fought three pigs and won. She still had four months to go. Jonathan and I were worried she'd just keep on growing, but Dorthea swore it was the cycle of life and that every cycle had an end.

"Why, Eula!" Momma howled. Excited as she was, I knew Momma was wondering where Cousin Eula's wedding band was. There isn't supposed to be no babies before marriage, even if the daddy was an exceptionally kind man, such as Barney.

As Momma's eyes drifted over her bare finger, Cousin Eula sputtered, "The wedding will be after the baby. That's how they do it now in the big cities."

We all knew there wasn't a bit of truth in that, but we let it go and focused on loving Cousin Eula for who she was, regardless of who she tried to be.

"I'm so hungry!" Cousin Eula whined. "I'm just going to grab a little snack from the kitchen." Patting Momma's leg over the comforter, she said, "I really hope you're feeling better. I'll come say goodbye before we leave, I promise."

And like an unexpected stink in the breeze, she was gone.

Momma and I giggled again.

"I know I give her a hard time," I recognized, "but I'm real happy for her."

"You are?"

I was a bit shocked. "Of course I am."

"I thought it might be hard for you, you know, watching everybody else fill their homes with babies."

"I told you time and time again, Momma, I'm okay. And I really mean that. My life is complete just the way it is. Rathe and I are blessed by the overwhelming amount of love in our lives. We have full hearts, Momma. It's time to stop fretting for me."

Momma cupped her hand over the top of mine on the bed. "All right."

"And it would be really nice if you came home with me for a while."

It didn't take Momma long to consider.

"You know," she said, "that would be real nice. Are you sure Luz wouldn't mind? There's not much room left at your place."

"It's the darnedest thing, Momma. Luz had taken up to helping me look after the Bakers. Not much time passed after that when Daryl took a shine to her. He's been working on a cottage on the Baker property ever since." Momma chuckled again, and I added, "Looks like it's gonna be a fall wedding."

"And Colin doesn't seem to mind?"

"He made true peace a long time ago, one day at a time." A smile started just in one corner, and spread across my lips faster than I could help. "Luz told me awhile back that she believes everyone's path in life is dependent on someone else's. I think hers relied on Widow Baker's. If it hadn't happened the way it did, her boys would never have the love that exists right now."

Taking a moment to think on it, Momma sat, eyes closed.

After a few minutes, I dared ask, "What do you think, Momma?"

"I'm sorry."

"For what?"

She took me by surprise.

"I was wrong. All those years ago, I was wrong telling

you nobody walked their own path. You always made your own."

"Momma—"

"Listen, I've been tough on you your whole life. Don't get me wrong, I'll do it till one of us turns to dust." Leaning upright, she confessed, "You and Shailene are the most glorious powers I ever knew, like great rivers. Maybe we're all rivers, racing each other, crossing one another. And if we're real lucky, our rivers flow together long enough to fill our hearts with the treasures of this fine world."

There. The fog had lifted in a rare moment when I got to see Momma not as my mother, but as a person, feeling her way through life like the rest of us.

"I believe I will visit your homestead for a spell. Tell your daddy to fetch my luggage. And lean forward a moment, will you."

I did as she asked. Before I could protest, she licked her palm and commenced to taming my hair with it.

"I just wish you'd brush your hair on occasion."

"It's laying straight, Momma."

"Always looks so wild. I'll be able to brush it every day for you, maybe more than once."

I didn't want to smile, but I couldn't help it.

After that, Momma came out to my house anytime she felt like death was upon her. Which, incidentally, proved to be every six to eight weeks for a number of years. Regardless, every visit, I always found time to say, "I'm glad you're here, Momma."

She treated Rathe with a gentler sense, and he took to her kinder demeanor like a pig took to mud. Daddy even showed his face every so often, bringing out anything he suspected we were low on. It wasn't to undermine Rathe's abilities, by any means. I think it was just Daddy's way of showing he cared.

We had all come so far to learn how to love each other well. I was proud of my family, and I contributed our strength to Shailene. If our paths hadn't crossed, we might never have found our love for one another, especially me and Momma. The last time Momma came to visit "sick," she really was. I held her hand every day, and we filled the hours with lifetimes. They were some of our best memories, along with those of our Shailene.

It made things feel right to know there was a little bit of Shailene still left in the world. Although I never knew where, I wished on a star for her baby every night.

EPILOGUE

I spent an ungodly amount of time mourning my sweet Shailene, feeling as though I'd lost the very best parts of myself to shadows and corrupt hearts. In doing so, however, I discovered the very best parts of everyone else. And so I lived my life true, loving everyone I could. Rathe and I had such wonderful years together, full of warm kitchen talks and even longer walks, bird watching and stealing kisses. And after Luz, Cousin Eula, and even Jonathan had handfuls of precious babies, I vowed to give everything I had and was to them, even leaving our wealth in their care when our footprints were long washed away. Because, for as many chances as you may have to sink a man, there are far more to lift one up.

My name's Nora Cravis, and I never left Granville County more than one day in my whole life because I had everything I ever wanted right here.

INSPIRATION FOR 'TIN MOON'

The inspiration for 'Tin Moon' originated from the following flash fiction work, 'And I Heard a Man Call My Name', which evolved from a writing prompt: The distance between two points increases over time.

And I Heard a Man Call My Name
by
Blakely Chorpenning

The distance between two points increases over time.

When I was fifteen, Daddy told me a story. He almost died once, when he was a little boy. There used to be a rope swing at the quarry. He must'a jumped that thing two thousand times that summer. Well, when two-thousand and one came around, his arm caught in the rope quicker than a mouse in the grip of a black snake. When the rope gave way, it smashed his child body into the rocks, breaking his arm and knocking him unconscious before he slipped into the water. Daddy's friends jumped in right away to save him. But he swore to me, before they pulled him free, a man called his name, clear as right next to him.

Daddy believed it was Death.

"Shailene," he said, "I'm telling you this because people squander their whole lives trying to figure out Death before he comes collecting."

I'll never forget that 'cause it felt like the only honest thing in a maze of fairy tales and hymns.

"Don't chase him. Just live true."

So I did. I tried hard to be the daughter they expected. Every evening after my homework, I helped Mama hand-stitch quilts. She would recite family stories I could tell my family one day. When I walked home from town, I always crossed sides when I reached the dirt road, where the older boys hung out to curse and hide from their chores. And when there was somewhere to be with my friends, I was there laughing with them, but I never fell to the gossip.

The distance between two points increases over time because human hearts don't know math, only "here" and "gone," and the life that fills the space between.

I was thinking of my daddy on the way home from town on a cool October day. The cows were out, the grass high. It looked like a painting in one of my sister's books. I only meant to stay for a little while, but the sun warmed my soul, and each dandelion called my name until I had enough stems to make necklaces for all my friends.

The light of day had almost drawn when I reached the dirt road. But I walked fast and stayed on my side. Only, when I passed by, the group of boys didn't stay on theirs.

I don't remember much. The world turned loud and ugly as they struck me, hitting and kicking, until the man in the moon dropped down and wept in my stead. Soon, all I knew was a coldness, like my body was a flesh sack filled with ice. My bones hurt as if they had splintered into a million jagged treacheries.

Until a quiet crept in as silent as a star in the night.

And I heard a man call my name.

SERIES & SINGLE TITLES BY BLAKELY CHORPENNING

Ell Clyne Series

(YA Paranormal Fiction)

A Madison Lark Adventure Series

(NA Shifter Fiction)

Hope & Darkness Series

(Dystopian Fiction)

Sinners & Saints Series

(Vampire Horror Fiction)

Literary Fiction:

Tin Moon

(Historical Fiction)

REVIEWS

Please take a moment to leave a review online. Your voice matters. By leaving a review, you can help fellow readers discover books by Blakely Chorpenning.

ABOUT THE AUTHOR

Blakely Chorpenning lives in the American South with the best family a woman could ask for. When she is not writing genre and literary fiction, Blakely and her family laugh a ton, craft more than any human should, and enjoy the little things.

Visit Blakely on:

Her Blog:
indiscriminatewrites.blogspot.com

Twitter:
@bchorpenning

Pinterest:
www.pinterest.com/bchorpenning

Facebook:
www.facebook.com/blakelychorpenning

Goodreads:
www.goodreads.com/author/show/5394681.Blakely_Chor-penning